JAMES STEPHENS

GW00707878

The Charwoman's Daughter

Introduction by Augustine Martin

Gill and Macmillan

Published by
Gill and Macmillan Ltd
Goldenbridge
Dublin 8
with associated companies in
London, New York, Delhi, Hong Kong,
Johannesburg, Lagos, Tokyo

First published by
Macmillan and Co. Ltd
London 1912

Cover design: Bill Murphy

7171 0633 0

Printed in Great Britain by
Richard Clay (The Chaucer Press) Ltd
Bungay, Suffolk

INTRODUCTION

Before its publication as a book in 1912 *The Charwoman's Daughter* ran as a serial in *The Irish Review* between April 1911 and February 1912 under the title *Mary, a Story*. The American edition of the book came out in the same year under the title *Mary, Mary*. Up to this point James Stephens had been comparatively unknown. He had published only one small volume of poems, *Insurrections*, three years previously. These poems had shown a certain crude energy, especially in their bitterness against the poverty and injustice of the world, but they had given little idea of the talent that was to emerge so dramatically in 1912, Stephens's *annus mirabilis;* because in that year he followed the success of *The Charwoman's Daughter* with his masterpiece of fantasy, *The Crock of Gold,* and a second volume of poetry, *The Hill of Vision.*

Stephens's origins are obscure. We know nothing for certain about his time or place of birth, his parents and early education. He claimed to have been born on the same day as James Joyce in 1882 and we have no option but to take his word for it. We know also that he spent some of his childhood in the slums of Dublin's north side and the rest of it in an orphanage, that he somehow learned typing, and that by the turn of the century he was working as a clerk in various Dublin offices and contributing poems and sketches to Arthur Griffith's paper, *Sinn Féin*. It was there that the poet A.E., George Russell, first saw his work and became convinced of his promise. In 1908 he called on Stephens at his office and took him into that circle of writers which had formed itself around Yeats and George Moore. It was the high point of the Irish

Literary Revival, and the stimulation of literary company seems to have encouraged Stephens and given him confidence in his powers. Within four years he was famous.

The Charwoman's Daughter is the first novel to deal with life in Dublin's slums. It is written by a man who lived in the midst of all that poverty and squalor, a poet who in his early work had expressed angry resentment at the lot of Dublin's poor. Eight years later he is to write a story entitled *Hunger* in which he shows how a working class family in Dublin starves to death, slowly and blamelessly. It is a stark, realistic story which carries a ferocious under-tow of social indignation. Yet, in *The Charwoman's Daughter*, the mood seems altogether free from personal and social bitterness. Though the details of the Makebelieves' tenement are given in vivid detail— the dark room, the dirty window, the decaying wallpaper, the carrying of water up five flights of stairs, the crippling poverty—the feeling one gets from a first reading is that of a supremely happy book. The squalid social realities are somehow transfigured by the idyllic mood of the narrative. Dublin's streets, parks and river, are vivid with sunlight. It has the quality of fairyland.

Here is Stephens's account of the book's genesis. In his essay 'On Prose and Verse' he tells how one day he was sadly pondering the only two possible themes for a novel, philosophy and murder, and his own incapacity to treat of either. He idly picks up Oscar Wilde's *The House of Pomegranates,* and, after reading twenty pages, he closes it because it has suddenly dawned on him that 'The art of prose writing does not really need a murder to carry it'. And that further :

> Writing can be quite good and have no violence whatever in it. It can be powerful on a minimum of action. It can be wise on a minimum of thought.

And so he concludes that both murder and philosophy are dispensable:

> I sat down forthwith in my one room, which contained my one new table, my one new wife, our brand new baby and our one large female mouse ... I looked at my wife and had immediately a model for Mary of this book. I looked within myself and found immediately my charwoman.

It is understandable that his wife, Cynthia, should have been the model for Mary Makebelieve, as she was the model for all his subsequent fictional heroines. He had met her at the age of seventeen and she was, apparently, very beautiful. Similarly, through the figure of the charwoman, he could channel a good deal of his own social anger as well as romantic dreams of a better world. But it is from Mary that the book takes its mood, its pervading atmosphere of wonder and excitement.

If one were to define the book's *genre* in strict literary terms one would call it a 'romance', the sort of novel that deals with an idealised world, with characters who are in one way or another above or beyond the ordinary using a tone which subdues the demands of strict realism. It might also be described in terms of the fairytale. In its salient features it retells the Cinderella story. Mary lives in the cinders but dreams, with the excessive support of her mother, of a better world. In the end she comes into her kingdom not by means of a social revolution but by the intervention of a sort of fairy uncle. And that is the proper outcome of a fairy story.

But within this fairytale framework Stephens manages to write a novel of considerable psychological insight. Briefly it might be looked upon in these ways: It is primarily a novel of growing up, of emerging from the world of childhood into the world of men and women. At the beginning Mary is a child inhabiting a totally female world. In her reveries by the pond in St Stephen's Green only one human relationship absorbs her, that of mother and child, as she watches the eels and the ducks. By the end of the book she has moved out into the world of adult experience and has learned to move there with emotional discrimination. The stages in the process are easily charted: one thinks of the moment when she first feels the threat and the challenge of the policeman's maleness; or the moment when in chapter 12 she turns impulsively at O'Connell Bridge towards the Phoenix Park, the area of adult experience, away from St Stephen's Green, the area of childhood innocence. This growing up is painful, and presented as such. It involves among other things a start in deception and dishonesty. It is painful for her mother who wants to keep her a child forever. Her mother, therefore, also grows up under the pressure of the novel's action.

It might be approached as a story about the tension between dream and reality, the intrusion of the one upon the other. By the end of the book Mary has seen the limitations of the dream and broken with it. Her mother is forced to do the same. This produces some of the best writing in the book, as for instance the painful scene in which the policeman comes to the Makebelieves' room in the tenement.

We can view it as a novel that deals unobtrusively and undidactically with class, the manner in which it can divide and humiliate: one thinks of Mrs Makebelieve tearing the dresses, of Mary on her knees in the O'Connor house, of Mary's evasiveness about her mother's way of life. This too is part of her process of growing up.

It might be seen also as a book that dramatises an obsessive theme in Stephens, the struggle of the male with the female principle. In his view the world is a system of polar opposites: day/night; good/evil; god/devil; man/woman. It follows that love between man and woman entails its opposite—hate. As the book opens the male, massively represented by the policeman, is having it all his own way. By the end the women have brought him to his knees. Remember how Mary wondered what it would be like to be hit by a man and her mother's reaction to this. The world is a clash of opposites in which power does not necessarily mean strength.

Perhaps it may be useful at moments to consider it as a picture of a city's life, public and private, and compare it with Joyce's Dublin as evidenced, say, in 'A Little Cloud', 'Two Gallants' and 'Eveline'. One could find no better example of the contrast between the quality of romance and realist fiction.

In *The Charwoman's Daughter* Stephens did more than write a strikingly mature first novel; in dealing effectively with working class Dublin he opened up an entirely new world for exploration. It is clear from the end note to the book that he intended a sequel. And years later, in Paris, he entertained the ambition to write a 'Comédie Humaine of Ireland', after the manner of Balzac. Instead he swerved towards fantasy, and within six months he had produced *The Crock of Gold*. For the rest of his career he is to be wrenched between the demands of realism and fantasy—a tension already present, as we have seen, in *The Charwoman's Daughter*. The chief and, perhaps, most regrettable casualty in this artistic conflict is the unfinished story of the Makebelieves and the tenement house they have just vacated. It is with genuine regret that we part from Mrs Cafferty with her tempestuous skirts and her halo of children, and from Mr Cafferty, dressed very comfortably in a red beard.

Augustine Martin

I

Mary Makebelieve lived with her mother in a small room at the very top of a big, dingy house in a Dublin back street. As long as she could remember she had lived in that top back room. She knew every crack in the ceiling, and they were numerous and of strange shapes. Every spot of mildew on the ancient wallpaper was familiar. She had, indeed, watched the growth of most from a greyish shade to a dark stain, from a spot to a great blob, and the holes in the skirting of the walls, out of which at night time the cockroaches came rattling, she knew also. There was but one window in the room, and when she wished to look out of it she had to push the window up, because the grime of many years had so encrusted the glass that it was of no more than the demi-semi-transparency of thin horn. When she did look there was nothing to see but a bulky array of chimney-pots crowning a next-door house, and these continually hurled jays of soot against her window; therefore, she did not care to look out often, for each time that she did so she was forced to wash herself, and as water had to be carried from the very bottom of the five-storey house up hundreds and hundreds of stairs to her room, she disliked having to use too much water.

Her mother seldom washed at all. She held that washing was very unhealthy and took the natural gloss off the face, and that, moreover, soap either tightened the skin or made it wrinkle. Her own face was very tight in some places and very loose in others, and Mary Makebelieve often thought that the tight places were spots which her mother used to wash when she was young, and the loose parts were those which had never

9

been washed at all. She thought that she would prefer
to be either loose all over her face or tight all over it,
and, therefore, when she washed she did it thoroughly,
and when she abstained she allowed of no compromise.

Her mother's face was the colour of old, old ivory.
Her nose was like a great strong beak, and on it the
skin was stretched very tightly, so that her nose shone
dully when the candle was lit. Her eyes were big and as
black as pools of ink and as bright as the eyes of a
bird. Her hair also was black, it was as smooth as the
finest silk, and when unloosened it hung straightly
down, shining about her ivory face. Her lips were thin
and scarcely coloured at all, and her hands were sharp,
quick hands, seeming all knuckle when she closed them
and all fingers when they were opened again.

Mary Makebelieve loved her mother very dearly, and
her mother returned her affection with an overwhelming passion that sometimes surged into physically painful caresses. When her mother hugged her for any
length of time she soon wept, rocking herself and her
daughter to and fro, and her clutch became then so
frantic that poor Mary Makebelieve found it difficult
to draw her breath; but she would not for the world
have disturbed the career of her mother's love. Indeed,
she found some pleasure in the fierceness of those
caresses, and welcomed the pain far more than she
reprobated it.

Her mother went out early every morning to work,
and seldom returned home until late at night. She was
a charwoman, and her work was to scrub out rooms
and wash down staircases. She also did cooking when
she was asked, and needlework when she got any to
do. She had made exquisite dresses which were worn
by beautiful young girls at balls and picnics, and fine
white shirts that great gentlemen wore when they were
dining, and fanciful waistcoats for gay young men, and
silk stockings for dancing in—but that was a long time
ago, because these beautiful things used to make her

angry when they were taken from her, so that she cursed the people who came to take them away, and sometimes tore up the dresses and danced on them and screamed.

She used often to cry because she was not rich. Sometimes, when she came home from work, she liked to pretend that she was rich; she would play at imagining that some one had died and left her a great fortune, or that her brother Patrick had come back from America with vast wealth, and then she would tell Mary Makebelieve of the things she intended to buy and do the very next day. Mary Makebelieve liked that . . . They were to move the first thing in the morning to a big house with a garden behind it full of fruit-trees and flowers and birds. There would be a wide lawn in front of the house to play lawn-tennis on, and to walk with delicately fine young men with fair faces and white hands, who would speak in the French language and bow often with their hats almost touching the ground. There were to be twelve servants—six of them men servants and six of them women servants—who would instantly do as they were bidden; and would receive ten shillings each per week and their board, and would also have two nights free in the week, and would be very well fed. There were many wonderful dresses for driving in a carriage, and others again for riding on horseback and for travelling in. There was a dress of crimson silk with a deep lace collar, and a heavy, wine-coloured satin dress with a gold chain falling down in front of it, and there was a pretty white dress of the finest linen, having one red rose pinned at the waist. There were black silken stockings with quaint designs worked on them in red silk, and scarves of silver gauze, and others embroidered with flowers and little shapes of men and women.

When her mother was planning all these things she was very happy, but afterwards she used to cry bitterly and rock her daughter to and fro on her breast until she hurt her.

2

Every morning about six o'clock Mary Makebelieve left her bed and lit the fire. It was an ugly fire to light, because the chimney had never been swept, and there was no draught. Also, they never had any sticks in the house, and scraps of paper twisted tightly into balls with the last night's cinders placed on them and a handful of small coals strewn on the top were used instead. Sometimes the fire blazed up quickly, and that made her happy, but at other times it went out three and four, and often half a dozen times; then the little bottle of paraffin oil had to be squandered—a few rags well steeped in the oil with a newspaper stretched over the grate seldom failed to coax enough fire to boil the saucepan of water; generally this method smoked the water, and then the tea tasted so horrid that one only drank it for the sake of economy.

Mrs Makebelieve liked to lie in bed until the last possible moment. As there was no table in the room Mary used to bring the two cups of tea, the tin of condensed milk, and the quarter of a loaf over to the bed, and there she and her mother took their breakfast.

From the time she opened her eyes in the morning her mother never ceased to talk. It was then she went over all the things that had happened on the previous day, and enumerated the places she would have to go to on the present day, and the chances for and against the making of a little money. At this meal she used to arrange also to have the room re-papered and the chimney swept and the rat-holes stopped up—there were three of these; one was on the left-hand side of the fire grate, the other two were under the bed, and Mary Makebelieve had lain awake many a night listening to the gnawing of teeth on the skirting and the scamper of

12

little feet here and there on the floor. Her mother further arranged to have a Turkey carpet placed on the floor, although she admitted that oilcloth or linoleum was easier to clean, but they were not so nice to the feet or the eye. Into all these improvements her daughter entered with the greatest delight. There was to be a red mahogany chest of drawers against one wall, and a rosewood piano against the wall opposite; a fender of shining brass, with brazen furniture, a bright copper kettle for boiling water in, and an iron pot for cooking potatoes and meat; there was to be a lifesized picture of Mary over the mantelpiece, and a picture of her mother near the window in a golden frame, also a picture of a Newfoundland dog lying in a barrel and a little wee terrier crawling up to make friends with him, and a picture of a battle between black people and soldiers.

Her mother knew it was time to get out of bed when she heard a heavy step coming from the next room and going downstairs. A labouring man lived there with his wife and six children. When the door banged she jumped up, dressed quickly, and flew from the room in a panic of haste. Usually then, as there was nothing to do, Mary went back to bed for another couple of hours. After this she rose, made the bed and tidied the room, and went out to walk in the streets, or to sit in the St Stephen's Green Park. She knew every bird in the Park, those that had chickens, and those that had had chickens, and those that never had any chickens at all—these latter were usually drakes, and had reason on their side for an abstention which might otherwise have appeared remarkable, but they did not deserve the pity which Mary lavished on their childlessness, nor the extra pieces of bread with which she sought to recompense them. She loved to watch the ducklings swimming after their mothers: they were quite fearless, and would dash to the water's edge where one was standing and pick up nothing with the greatest eagerness and swallow it with delight. The mother duck swam placidly close to her brood, and clucked in a low voice all kinds of warnings and advice and reproof to the little ones. Mary Makebelieve thought it was very clever of the little ducklings to be able to swim so well. She loved them, and when nobody was looking she used to cluck at them like their mother; but she did not often do this, because she did not know duck language really well, and feared that her cluck might mean the wrong things, and that she might be giving these innocents bad advice, and telling them to do something contrary to what their mother had just directed.

The bridge across the big lake was a fascinating place. On the sunny side lots of ducks were always standing on their heads searching for something in the water, so that they looked like only half ducks. On the shady side hundreds of eels were swimming about—they were most wonderful things: some of them were thin like ribbons, and others were round and plump like thick ropes. They never seemed to fight at all, and although the ducklings were so tiny the big eels never touched any of them, even when they dived right down amongst them. Some of the eels swam along very slowly, looking on this side and on that as if they were out of work or up from the country, and others whizzed by with incredible swiftness. Mary Makebelieve thought that the latter kind had just heard their babies crying; she wondered, when a little fish cried, could its mother see the tears where there was already so much water about, and then she thought that maybe they cried hard lumps of something that was easily visible.

After this she would go around the flowerbeds and look at each; some of them were shaped like stars, and some were quite round, and others again were square. She liked the star-shaped flowerbeds best, and next she liked the round ones, and last of all the square. But she loved all the flowers, and used to make up stories about them.

After that, growing hungry, she would go home for

her lunch. She went home down Grafton Street and O'Connell Street. She always went along the right-hand side of the street going home, and looked in every shop window that she passed; and then, when she had eaten her lunch, she came out again and walked along the left-hand side of the road, looking at the shops on that side; and so she knew daily everything that was new in the city, and was able to tell her mother at night time that the black dress with Spanish lace was taken out of Manning's window, and a red gown with tucks at the shoulders and Irish lace at the wrists put in its place; or that the diamond ring in Johnson's marked One Hundred Pounds was gone from the case, and that a slide of brooches of beaten silver and blue enamel was there instead.

In the night time her mother and herself went round to each of the theatres in turn and watched the people going in, and looked at the big posters. When they went home afterwards they had supper, and used to try to make out the plots of the various plays from the pictures they had seen, so that generally they had lots to talk about before they went to bed. Mary Makebelieve used to talk most in the night time, but her mother talked most in the morning

3

Her mother spoke sometimes of matrimony as a thing remote but very certain : the remoteness of this adventure rather shocked Mary Makebelieve; she knew that a girl had to get married, that a strange, beautiful man would come from somewhere looking for a wife, and would retire again with his bride to that Somewhere which is the country of Romance. At times (and she could easily picture it) he rode in armour on a great bay horse, the plume of his helmet trailing among the high leaves of the forest. Or he came standing on the prow of a swift ship with the sunlight blazing back from his golden armour. Or on a grassy plain, fleet as the wind, he came running, leaping, laughing.

When the subject of matrimony was under discussion her mother planned minutely the person of the groom, his vast accomplishments, and yet vaster wealth, the magnificence of his person, and the love in which he was held by rich and poor alike. She also discussed, down to the smallest detail, the elaborate trousseau she would provide for her daughter, the extravagant presents the bridegroom would make to his bride and her maids, and those, yet more costly, which the bridegroom's family would send to the newly-married pair. All these wonders could only concentrate in the person of a lord. Mary Makebelieve's questions as to the status and appurtenances of a lord were searching and minute; her mother's rejoinders were equally elaborate and particular.

At his birth a lord is cradled in silver; at his death he is laid in a golden casket, an oaken coffin, and a leaden outer coffin, until, finally, a massy stone sarcophagus shrouds his remains for ever. His life is a whirl of gaiety and freedom. Around his castle there spreads miles upon miles of sunny grass lands and ripened orchards and waving forests, and through these he hunts with his laughing companions or walks gently with his lady. He has servants by the thousand, each anxious to die for him, and his wealth, prodigious beyond the computation of avarice, is stored in underground chambers, whose low, tortuous passages lead to labyrinths of vaults massy and impregnable.

Mary Makebelieve would have loved to wed a lord. If a lord had come to her when she paced softly through a forest, or stood alone on the seashore, or crouched among the long grass of a windy plain, she would have placed her hands in his and followed him and loved him truly for ever. But she did not believe that these things

16

happened nowadays, nor did her mother. Nowadays! Her mother looked on these paltry times with an eye whose scorn was complicated by fury. Mean, ugly days! mean, ugly lives! and mean, ugly people! said her mother, that's all one can get nowadays; and then she spoke of the people whose houses she washed out and whose staircases she scrubbed down, and her old-ivory face flamed from her black hair, and her deep, dark eyes whirled and became hard and motionless as points of jet, and her hands jumped alternately into knuckles and claws.

But it became increasingly evident to Mary Make-believe that marriage was not a story but a fact, and, somehow, the romance of it did not drift away, although the very house wherein she lived was infested by these conjoints, and the streets wherein she walked were crowded with undistinguished couples. . . . Those grey-lived, dreary-natured people had a spark of fire smouldering somewhere in their poor economy. Six feet deep is scarcely deep enough to bury romance, and until that depth of clay has clogged our bones the fire can still smoulder and be fanned, and, perhaps, blaze up and flare across a county or a country to warm the cold hands of many a shrivelled person.

How did all these people come together? She did not yet understand the basic necessity that drives the male to the female. Sex was not yet to her a physiological distinction, it was only a differentiation of clothing, a matter of whiskers and no whiskers : but she had begun to take a new and peculiar interest in men. One of these hurrying or loitering strangers might be the husband whom fate had ordained for her. She would scarcely have been surprised if one of the men who looked at her casually in the street had suddenly halted and asked her to marry him. It came on her with something like assurance that that was the only business these men were there for; she could not discover any other reason or excuse for their existence, and if some man had been

17

thus adventurous Mary Makebelieve would have been sadly perplexed to find an answer: she might, indeed, have replied, "Yes, thank you, sir," for when a man asks one to do a thing for him one does it gladly. There was an attraction about young men which she could not understand, something peculiarly dear and magnetic; she would have liked to shake hands with one to see how different he felt from a girl. They would, probably, shake hands quite hard and then hit one. She fancied she would not mind being hit by a man, and then, watching the vigour of their movements, she thought they could hit very hard, but still there was a terrible attraction about the idea of being hit by a man. She asked her mother (with apparent irrelevance), had a man ever struck her? Her mother was silent for a few moments, and then burst into so violent a passion of weeping that Mary Makebelieve was frightened. She rushed into her mother's arms, and was rocked fiercely against a heart almost bursting with bitter pride and recollection. But her mother did not then, nor did she ever afterwards, answer Mary Makebelieve's question.

4

Every afternoon a troop of policemen marched in solemn and majestic single file from the College Green Police Station. At regular intervals, one by one, a policeman stepped sideways from the file, adjusted his belt, touched his moustache, looked up the street and down the street for stray criminals, and condescended to the duties of his beat.

At the crossing where Nassau and Suffolk Streets intersect Grafton Street one of these superb creatures was wont to relinquish his companions, and there in the centre of the road, a monument of solidarity and law, he remained until the evening hour which released him again to the companionship of his peers.

Perhaps this point is the most interesting place in Dublin. Upon one vista Grafton Street with its glittering shops stretches, or rather winds, to the St Stephen's Green Park, terminating at the gate known as the Fusiliers' Arch, but which local patriotism has rechristened the Traitors' Gate. On the left Nassau Street, broad and clean, and a trifle vulgar and bourgeois in its openness, runs away to Merrion Square, and on with a broad ease to Blackrock and Kingstown and the sea. On the right hand Suffolk Street, reserved and shy, twists up to St Andrew's Church, touches gingerly the South City Markets, droops to George's Street, and is lost in mean and dingy intersections. At the back of the crossing Grafton Street continues again for a little distance down to Trinity College (at the gates whereof very intelligent young men flaunt very tattered gowns and smoke massive pipes with great skill for their years), skirting the Bank of Ireland, and on to the River Liffey and the street which local patriotism defiantly speaks of as O'Connell Street, and alien patriotism, with equal defiance and pertinacity, knows as Sackville Street.

To the point where these places meet, and where the policeman stands, all the traffic of Dublin converges in a constant stream. The trams hurrying to Terenure, or Donnybrook, or Dalkey flash around this corner; the doctors, who, in these degenerate days, concentrate in Merrion Square, fly up here in carriages and motor-cars; the vans of the great firms in Grafton and O'Connell Streets, or those outlying, never cease their exuberant progress. The ladies and gentlemen of leisure stroll here daily at four o'clock, and from all sides the vehicles and pedestrians, the bicycles and motor bicycles, the trams and the outside cars rush to the solitary policeman, who directs them all with his severe but tolerant eye. He knows all the tram-drivers who go by, and his nicely graduated wink rewards the glances of the rubicund, jolly drivers of the hackneys and the decayed jehus with purple faces and dismal hopefulness who drive sepulchral cabs for some reason which has no acquaintance with profit; nor are the ladies and gentlemen who saunter past foreign to his encyclopedic eye. Constantly his great head swings a slow recognition, constantly his serene finger motions onwards a well-known undesirable, and his big white teeth flash for an instant at young, laughing girls and the more matronly acquaintances who solicit the distinction of his glance.

To this place, and about this hour, Mary Makebelieve, returning from her solitary lunch, was wont to come. The figure of the massive policeman fascinated her. Surely everything desirable in manhood was concentrated in his tremendous body. What an immense, shattering blow that mighty fist could give! She could imagine it swinging vast as the buffet of a hero, high-thrown and then down irresistibly—a crashing, monumental hand. She delighted in his great, solid head as it swung slowly from side to side, and his calm, proud eye—a governing, compelling, and determined eye. She had never met his glance yet : she withered away before it as a mouse withers and shrinks and falls to its den before a cat's huge glare. She used to look at him from the kerbstone in front of the chemist's shop, or on the opposite side of the road, while pretending to wait for a tram; and at the pillar-box beside the optician's she found time for one furtive twinkle of a glance that shivered to his face and trembled away into the traffic. She did not think he noticed her; but there was nothing he did not notice. His business was noticing : he caught her in his mental policeman's notebook the very first day she came; he saw her each day beside, and at last looked for her coming and enjoyed her strategy. One day her shy, creeping glance was caught by his; it held her mesmerised for a few seconds; it looked down into her—for a moment the whole world seemed to have become one immense eye —she could scarcely get away from it.

20

When she remembered again she was standing by the pond in the St Stephen's Green Park, with a queer, frightened exaltation lightening through her blood. She did not go home that night by Grafton Street—she did not dare venture within reach of that powerful organism —but went a long way round, and still the way seemed very short.

That night her mother, although very tired, was the more talkative of the two. She offered in exchange for her daughter's thoughts pennies that only existed in her imagination. Mary Makebelieve professed that it was sleep and not thought obsessed her, and exhibited voucher yawns which were as fictitious as her reply. When they went to bed that night it was a long time before she slept. She lay looking into the deep gloom of the chamber, and scarcely heard the fierce dreams of her mother, who was demanding from a sleep world the things she lacked in the wide-awake one.

5

This is the appearance was on Mary Makebelieve at that time : she had fair hair, and it was very soft and very thick; when she unwound this it fell, or rather flowed, down to her waist, and when she walked about her room with her hair unloosened it curved beautifully about her head, snuggled into the hollow of her neck, ruffled out broadly again upon her shoulders, and swung into and out of her figure with every motion, surging and shrink-ing and dancing; the ends of her hair were soft and loose as foam, and it had the colour and shining of pure, light gold. Commonly in the house she wore her hair loose, because her mother liked the appearance of youth imparted by hanging hair, and would often desire her daughter to leave off her outer skirt and walk only in her petticoats to heighten the illusion of girlishness. Her head was shaped very tenderly and softly; it was so small that when her hair was twisted up it seemed much too delicate to bear so great a burden. Her eyes were grey, limpidly tender and shy, drooping under weighty lids, so that they seldom seemed more than half opened, and commonly sought the ground rather than the bolder excursions of straightforwardness; they seldom looked for longer than a glance, climbing and poising and eddying about the person at whom she gazed, and then dived away again; and always when she looked at any one she smiled a deprecation of her boldness. She had a small white face, very like her mother's in some ways and at some angles, but the tight beak which was her mother's nose was absent in Mary; her nose withdrew timidly in the centre, and only snatched a hurried courage to become visible at the tip. It was a nose which seemed to have been snubbed almost out of existence. Her mother loved it because it was so little, and had tried so hard not to be a nose at all. They often stood together before the little glass that had a great crack running drunkenly from the right-hand top corner down to the left-hand bottom corner, and two small arm crosses, one a little above the other, in the centre. Where one's face looked into this glass it often appeared there as four faces with horrible aberrations; an ear might be curving around a lip, or an eye leering strangely in the middle of a chin. But there were ways of looking into the glass which practice had discovered, and usage had long ago dulled the terrors of its vagaries. Looking into this glass, Mrs Makebelieve would comment minutely upon the two faces therein, and, pointing to her own triumphantly genuine nose and the fact that her husband's nose had been of quite discernible proportions, she would seek in labyrinths of pedigree for a reason to justify her daughter's lack; she passed all her sisters in this review, with an army of aunts and great-aunts, rifling tombs of grandparents and their remoter blood, and making long-dead noses to live again. Mary Makebelieve used to lift her timidly curious eye and smile in deprecation of her nasal shortcomings, and then her mother would kiss the dejected button and vow it was the dearest, loveliest bit of a nose that had ever been seen.

'Big noses suit some people,' said Mrs Makebelieve, 'but they do not suit others, and one would not suit you, dearie. They go well with black-haired people and very tall people, military gentlemen, judges and apothecaries; but, small, fair folk cannot support great noses. I like my own nose,' she continued. 'At school, when I was a little girl, the other girls used to laugh at my nose, but I always liked it, and after a time other people came to like it also.'

Mary Makebelieve had small, slim hands and feet: the palms of her hands were softer than anything in the world; there were five little, pink cushions on her palm —beginning at the little finger there was a very tiny cushion, the next one was bigger, and the next bigger again, until the largest ended a perfect harmony at the base of her thumb. Her mother used to kiss these little cushions at times, holding back the finger belonging to each, and naming it as she touched it. These are the names of Mary Makebelieve's fingers, beginning with the thumb: Tom Tumkins, Willie Winkles, Long Daniel, Bessie Bobtail, and Little Dick-Dick.

Her slight, girlish figure was only beginning to creep to the deeper contours of womanhood, a half curve here and there, a sudden softness in the youthful lines, certain angles trembling on the slightest of rolls, a hint, a suggestion, the shadowy prophecy of circles and half hoops that could not yet roll: the trip of her movements was troubled sometimes to a sedater motion.

These things her mother's curiosity was continually recording, sometimes with happy pride, but oftener in a kind of anger to find that her little girl was becoming a big girl. If it had been possible she would have detained her daughter for ever in the physique of a child; she feared the time when Mary would become too evidently a woman, when all kinds of equalities would come to hinder her spontaneous and active affection. A woman might object to be nursed, while a girl would not; Mrs Makebelieve feared that objection, and, indeed, Mary, under the stimulus of an awakening body and a new, strange warmth, was not altogether satisfied by being nursed or by being the passive participant in these caresses. She sometimes thought that she would like to take her mother on her own breast and rock her to and fro, crooning soft made-up words and kissing the top of a head or the half-hidden curve of a cheek, but she did not dare to do so for fear her mother would strike her. Her mother was very jealous on that point; she loved her daughter to kiss her and stroke her hands and her face, but never liked her to play at being the mother, nor had she ever encouraged her daughter in the occupations of a doll. She was the mother and Mary was the baby, and she could not bear to have her motherhood hindered even in play.

6

Although Mary Makebelieve was sixteen years of age she had not yet gone to work; her mother did not like the idea of her little girl stooping to the drudgery of the only employment she could have aided her to obtain—that was, to assist herself in the humble and arduous toil of charring. She had arranged that Mary was to go into a shop, a drapery store, or some such other, but that was to be in a sometime which seemed infinitely remote. 'And then, too,' said Mrs Makebelieve, 'all kinds of things may happen in a year or so if we wait. Your uncle Patrick, who went to America twenty years ago, may come home, and when he does you will not have to work, dearie, nor will I. Or again, some one going along the street may take a fancy to you and marry you; things often happen like that.' There were a thousand schemes and accidents which, in her opinion, might occur to the establishment of her daughter's ease and the enlargement of her own dignity. And so Mary Makebelieve, when her mother was at work (which was sometimes every day in the week) had all the day to loiter in and spend as best she liked. Sometimes she did not go out at all. She stayed in the top back room sewing or knitting, mending holes in the sheets or the blankets, or reading books from the Free Library in Capel Street : but generally she preferred, after the few hours which served to put the room in order, to go out and walk along the streets, taking new turnings as often as she fancied, and striking down strange roads to see the shops and the people.

There were so many people whom she knew by sight; almost daily she saw these somewhere, and she often followed them for a short distance, with a feeling of friendship; for the loneliness of the long day often drew down upon her like a weight, so that even the distant companionship of these remembered faces that did not know her was comforting. She wished she could find out who some of them were. There was a tall man with a sweeping brown beard, whose heavy overcoat looked as though it had been put on with a shovel; he wore spectacles, and his eyes were blue, and always seemed as if they were going to laugh; he, also, looked into the shops as he went along, and he seemed to know everybody. Every few paces people would halt and shake his hand, but these people never spoke, because the big man with the brown beard would instantly burst into a fury of speech which had no intervals; and when there was no one with him at all he would talk to himself. On these occasions he did not see any one, and people had to jump out of his way while he strode onwards swinging his big head from one side to the other, and with his eyes fixed on some place a great distance away. Once or twice, in passing, she heard him singing to himself the most lugubrious song in the world. There was another— a long, thin, black man—who looked young and was always smiling secretly to himself; his lips were never still for a moment, and, passing Mary Makebelieve a few times, she heard him buzzing like a great bee. He did not stop to shake hands with any one, and although many people saluted him he took no heed, but strode on, smiling his secret smile and buzzing serenely. There was a third man whom she often noticed : his clothing seemed as if it had been put on him a long time ago and had never been taken off again. He had a long, pale face, with a dark moustache drooping over a most beautiful mouth. His eyes were very big and lazy, and did not look quite human; they had a trick of looking sidewards—a most intimate, personal look. Sometimes he saw nothing in the world but the pavement, and at other times he saw everything. He looked at Mary Makebelieve once, and she got a fright; she had a queer idea that she had known him well hundreds of years before, and that he remembered her also. She was afraid of that man, but she liked him because he looked so gentle and so—there was something else he looked which as yet she could not put a name to, but which her ancestry remembered dimly. There was a short, fair, pale-faced man, who looked like the tiredest man in the world. He was often preoccupied, but not in the singular way the others were. He seemed to be always chewing the cud of remembrance, and looked at people as if they reminded him of other people who were dead a long time and whom he thought of but did not regret. He was a detached man even in a crowd, and carried with him a cold atmosphere; even his smile was bleak and aloof. Mary Makebelieve noticed that many people nudged each other as he went by, and then they would turn and look after him and go away whispering.

These and many others she saw almost daily, and used

26

to look for with a feeling of friendship. At other times she walked up the long line of quays sentinelling the Liffey, watching the swift boats of Guinness puffing down the river, and the thousands of sea-gulls hovering above or swimming on the dark waters, until she came to the Phoenix Park, where there was always a cricket or football match being played, or some young men or girls playing hurley, or children playing tip-and-tig, running after one another, and dancing and screaming in the sunshine. Her mother liked very much to go with her to the Phoenix Park on days when there was no work to be done. Leaving the great, white main road, up which the bicycles and motor-cars are continually whizzing, a few minutes' walk brings one to quiet alleys sheltered by trees and groves of hawthorn. In these passages one can walk for a long time without meeting a person, or lie on the grass in the shadow of a tree and watch the sunlight beating down on the green fields and shimmering between the trees. There is a deep silence to be found here, very strange and beautiful to one fresh from the city, and it is strange also to look about in the broad sunshine and see no person near at all, and no movement saving the roll and folding of the grass, the slow swinging of the branches of the trees, or the noiseless flight of a bee, a butterfly, or a bird.

These things Mary Makebelieve liked, but her mother would pine for the dances of the little children, the gallant hurrying of the motor-cars, and the movement to and fro of the people with gay dresses and coloured parasols and all the circumstance of holiday.

7

One morning Mary Makebelieve jumped out of bed and lit the fire. For a wonder it lit easily: the match was scarcely applied when the flames were leaping up the black chimney, and this made her feel at ease with the world. Her mother stayed in bed chatting with something more of gaiety than usual. It was nearly six o'clock, and the early summer sun was flooding against the grimy window. The previous evening's post had brought a postcard for Mrs Makebelieve, requesting her to call on a Mrs O'Connor, who had a house off Harcourt Street. This, of course, meant a day's work—it also meant a new client.

Mrs Makebelieve's clients were always new. She could not remain for any length of time in people's employment without being troubled by the fact that these folk had houses of their own and were actually employing her in a menial capacity. She sometimes looked at their black silk aprons in a way which they never failed to observe with anger, and on their attempting (as they always termed it) to put her in her proper place, she would discuss their appearance and morals with such power that they at once dismissed her from their employment and incited their husbands to assault her.

Mrs Makebelieve's mind was exercised in finding out who had recommended her to this new lady, and in what terms of encomium such recommendation had been framed. She also debated as to whether it would be wise to ask for one shilling and ninepence per day instead of the customary one shilling and sixpence. If the house was a big one she might be required by this new customer oftener than once a week, and, perhaps, there were others in the house besides the lady who would find small jobs for her to do—needlework or messages, or some such which would bring in a little extra money; for she professed her willingness and ability to undertake with success any form of work in which a woman could be eminent. In a house where she had worked she had once been asked by a gentleman who lodged there to order in two dozen bottles of stout, and, on returning with the stout, the gentleman had thanked her and given her a shilling. Incidents parallel to this had kept her faith in humanity green. There must be plenty of these open-handed gentlemen in houses such as she worked in, and, perhaps, in Mrs O'Connor's house there might be more than one such person. There were stingy people enough, heaven knew, people who would get one to run messages and almost expect to be paid themselves for allowing one to work for them. Mrs Makebelieve anathematised such skinflints with a vocabulary which was quite equal to the detailing of their misdeeds; but she refused to dwell on them : they were not really important in a world where the sun was shining. In the night time she would again believe in their horrible existences, but until then the world must be peopled with kind-hearted folk. She instanced many whom she knew, people who had advanced services and effects without exacting or indeed expecting any return.

When the tea was balanced insecurely on the bed, the two tea-cups on one side of her legs, the three-quarters of a loaf and the tin of condensed milk on the other, Mary sat down with great care, and all through the breakfast her mother culled from her capacious memory a list of kindnesses of which she had been the recipient or the witness. Mary supplemented the recital by incidents from her own observation. She had often seen a man in the street give a penny to an old woman. She had often seen old women give things to other old women. She knew many people who never looked for the halfpenny change from a newsboy. Mrs Makebelieve applauded the justice of such transactions; they were, she admitted, the things she would do herself if she were in a position to be careless; but a person to whom the discovery of her daily bread is a daily problem, and who can scarcely keep pace with the ever-changing terms of the problem, is not in a position to be careless. 'Grind, grind, grind,' said Mrs Makebelieve, 'that is life for me, and if I ceased to grind for an instant . . .' she flickered

29

her thin hand into a nowhere of terror. Her attitude was, that when one had enough one should give the residue to some one who had not enough. It was her woe, it stabbed her to the heart, to see desolate people dragging through the streets, standing to glare through the windows of bakeries and confectioners' shops, and little children in some of these helpless arms! Thinking of these, she said that every morsel she ate would choke her were it not for her own hunger. But maybe, said she, catching a providential glance of the golden-tinted window, maybe these poor people were not as poor as they seemed : surely they had ways of collecting a living which other people did not know anything about. It might be that they got lots of money from kind-hearted people, and food at hospitable doors, and here and there clothing and oddments which, if they did not wear, they knew how to dispose of advantageously. What extremes of ways and means such people must be acquainted with! No ditch was too low to be ravaged; a gate represented something to be climbed over; an open door was an invitation, a locked one a challenge. They could dodge under the fences of the law and climb the barbed wire of morality with equal impunity, and the utmost rigour of punishment had little terror for those whose hardships could scarcely be artificially worsened. The stagger of despair, the stricken, helpless aspect of such people, their gaunt faces and blurred eyes, might conceivably be their stock-in-trade, the keys wherewith they unlocked hearts and purses and area doors. It must be so when the sun was shining and birds were singing across fields not immeasurably distant, and children in walled gardens romped among fruits and flowers. She would believe this, for it was the early morning when one must believe, but when the night time came again she would laugh to scorn such easy beliefs, she would see the lean ribs of humanity when she undressed herself.

8

After her mother had gone, Mary Makebelieve occupied herself settling the room and performing the various offices which the keeping in order of even one small room involves. There were pieces of the wallpaper flapping loosely; these had to be gummed down with strips of stamp-paper. The bed had to be made, the floor scrubbed, and a miscellany of objects patted and tapped into order. Her few dresses also had to be gone over for loose buttons, and the darning of threadbare places was a duty exercising her constant attention. Her clothing was always made by her mother, whose needle had once been noted for expertness, and, therefore, fitted more accurately than is customary in young girls' dresses. The arranging and rearranging of her beads was a frequent and enjoyable labour. She had four different necklaces, representing four different pennyworths of beads purchased at a shop whose merchandise was sold for one penny per item. One pennyworth of these beads was coloured green, another red, a third was coloured like pearls, and the fourth was a miscellaneous packet of many colours. A judicious selection of these beads could always provide a new and magnificent necklace at the expense of little more than a half-hour's easy work.

Because the sun was shining she brought out her white dress, and for a time was busy on it. There had been five tucks in the dress, but one after one they had to be let out. This was the last tuck that remained, and it also had to go, but even with such extra lengthening the dress would still swing free of her ankles. Her mother had promised to add a false hem to it when she got time, and Mary determined to remind her of this promise as soon as she came in from work. She polished her shoes, put on the white dress, and then did up her hair in front of the cracked looking-glass. She always put up her hair very plainly. She first combed it down straight, then parted it in the centre, and rolled it into a great ball at the back of her neck. She often wished to curl her hair, and, indeed, it would have curled with the lightest persuasion; but her mother, being approached on the subject, said that curls were common and were seldom worn by respectable people, excepting very small children or actresses, both of whose slender mentalities were registered by these tiny daintinesses. Also, curls took up too much time in arranging, and the slightest moisture in the air was liable to draw them down into lank and unsightly plasters, and, therefore, saving for a dance or a picnic, curls should not be used.

Mary Makebelieve, having arranged her hair, hesitated for some time in the choice of a necklace. There was the pearl-coloured necklace—it was very pretty, but every one could tell at once that they were not genuine pearls. Real pearls of the bigness of these would be very valuable. Also, there was something childish about pearls which latterly she wished to avoid. She had quite grown up now. The letting down of the last tuck in her dress marked an epoch as distinct as did the first rolling up of her hair. She wished her dress would go right down to her heels so that she might have a valid reason for holding up her skirts with one hand. She felt a trifle of impatience because her mother had delayed making the false hem : she could have stitched it on herself if her mother had cut it out, but for this day the dress would have to do. She wished she owned a string of red coral; not that round beady sort, but the jagged criss-cross coral—a string of these long enough to go twice round her neck, and yet hang down in front to her waist. If she owned a string as long as that she might be able to cut enough off to make a slender wristlet. She would have loved to see such a wristlet sagging down to her hand.

Red, it seemed, would have to be the colour for this

day, so she took the red beads out of a box and put them on. They looked very nice against her white dress, but still—she did not quite like them : they seemed too solid, so she put them back into the box again, and instead tied round her neck a narrow ribbon of black velvet, which satisfied her better. Next she put on her hat; it was of straw, and had been washed many times. There was a broad ribbon of black velvet around it. She wished earnestly that she had a sash of black velvet about three inches deep to go round her waist. There was such a piece about the hem of her mother's Sunday skirt, but, of course, that could not be touched; maybe her mother would give it to her if she asked. The skirt would look quite as well without it, and when her mother knew how nice it looked round her waist she would certainly give it to her.

She gave a last look at herself in the glass and went out, turning up to the quays in the direction of the Phoenix Park. The sun was shining gloriously, and the streets seemed wonderfully clean in the sunlight. The horses under the heavy drays pulled their loads as if they were not heavy. The big, red-faced drivers leaned back at ease, with their hard hats pushed back from their foreheads and their eyes puckered at the sunshine. The tram-cars whizzed by like great jewels. The outside cars went spanking down the broad road, and every jolly-faced jarvey winked at her as he jolted by. The people going up and down the street seemed contented and happy. It was one o'clock, and from all kinds of offices and shops young men and women were darting forth for their lunch; none of the young men were so hurried but they had a moment to glance admiringly at Mary Make-believe before diving into a cheap restaurant or cheaper public-house for their food. The gulls in the river were flying in long, lazy curves, dipping down to the water, skimming it an instant, and then wheeling up again with easy, slanting wings. Every few minutes a boat laden with barrels puffed swiftly from beneath a bridge. All these boats had pretty names—there was the *Shannon*, the *Suir*, the *Nore*, the *Lagan*, and many others. The men on board sat contentedly on the barrels and smoked and made slow remarks to one another; and overhead the sky was blue and wonderful, immeasurably distant, filled from horizon to horizon with sparkle and warmth. Mary Makebelieve went slowly on towards the Park. She felt very happy. Now and then a darker spot flitted through her mind, not at all obscuring, but toning the brightness of her thoughts to a realisable serenity. She wished her skirts were long enough to be held up languidly like the lady walking in front : the hand holding up the skirt had a golden curb-chain on the wrist which drooped down to the neatly-gloved hand, and between each link of the chain was set a blue turquoise, and upon this jewel the sun danced splendidly. Mary Makebelieve wished she had a slender red coral wristlet; it also would have hung down to her palm and been lovely in the sunlight, and it would, she thought, have been far nicer than the bangle.

9

She walked along for some time in the Park. Through the railings flanking the great road many beds of flowers could be seen. These were laid out in a great variety of forms, of stars and squares and crosses and circles, and the flowers were arranged in exquisite patterns. There was a great star which flamed with red flowers at the deep points, and in its heart a heavier mass of yellow blossom glared suddenly. There were circles wherein each ring was a differently-coloured flower, and others where three rings alternated—three rings white, three purple, and three orange, and so on in slenderer circles to the tiniest diminishing. Mary Makebelieve wished she knew the names of all the flowers, but the only ones she recognised by sight were the geraniums, some species of roses, violets, and forget-me-nots and pansies. The more exotic sorts she did not know, and, while she admired them greatly, she had not the same degree of affection for them as for the commoner, friendly varieties.

Leaving the big road, she wandered into wider fields. In a few moments the path was hidden; the outside cars, motor-cars, and bicycles had vanished as completely as though there were no such things in the world. Great numbers of children were playing about in distinct bands; each troop was accompanied by one and sometimes two older people, girls or women who lay stretched out on the warm grass or leaned against the tree-trunks reading novelettes, and around them the children whirled and screamed and laughed. It was a world of waving pinafores and thin, black-stockinged legs and shrill, sweet voices. In the great spaces the children's voices had a strangely remote quality; the sweet, high tones were not such as one heard in the streets or in houses. In a house or a street these voices thudded upon the air and beat sonorously back again from the walls, the houses, or the pavements; but out here the slender sounds sang to a higher tenuity and disappeared out and up and away into the tree-tops and the clouds and the wide, windy reaches. The little figures partook also of this diminuendo effect; against the great grassy curves they seemed smaller than they really were; the trees stirred hugely above them, the grass waved vast beneath them, and the sky ringed them in from immensity. Their forms scarcely disturbed the big outline of nature; their laughter only whispered against the silence, as ineffectual to disturb that gigantic serenity as a gnat's wing fluttered against a precipice.

Mary Makebelieve wandered on; a few cows lifted solemnly curious faces as she passed, and swung their heavy heads behind her. Once or twice half a dozen deer came trotting from beyond the trees, and were shocked

35

to a halt on seeing her—a moment's gaze, and away like the wind, bounding in a delicious freedom. Now a butterfly came twisting on some eccentric journey—ten wingbeats to the left, twenty to the right, and then back to the left, or, with a sudden twist, returning on the path which it had already traversed, jerking carelessly through the sunlight. Across the sky, very far up, a troop of birds sailed definitely—they knew where they were going; momentarily one would detach itself from the others in a burst of joyous energy and sweep a great circle and back again to its comrades, and then away, away, away to the skyline.—Ye swift ones! O, freedom and sweetness! A song falling from the heavens! A lilt through deep sunshine! Happy wanderers! How fast ye fly and how bravely—up and up, till the earth has fallen away and the immeasurable heavens and the deep loneliness of the sunlight and the silence of great spaces receive you!

Mary Makebelieve came to a tree around which a circular wooden seat had been placed. Here for a time she sat looking out on the wide fields. Far away in front the ground rolled down into valleys and up into little hills, and from the valleys the green heads of trees emerged, and on the further hills, in slender, distinct silhouette, and in great masses, entire trees could be seen. Nearer were single trees, each with its separate shadow and a stream of sunlight flooding between; and everywhere the greenery of leaves and of grass, and the gold of myriad buttercups, and multitudes of white daisies.

She had been sitting for some time when a shadow came from behind her. She watched its lengthening and its queer bobbing motion. When it grew to its greatest length it ceased to move. She felt that some one had stopped. From the shape of the shadow she knew it was a man, but being so close she did not like to look. Then a voice spoke. It was a voice as deep as the rolling of a sea.

'Hello,' said the voice, 'what are you doing here alone, young lady?'

Mary Makebelieve's heart suddenly spurted to full speed. It seemed to want more space than her bosom could afford. She looked up. Beside her stood a prodigious man : one lifted hand curled his moustache, the other carelessly twirled a long cane. He was dressed in ordinary clothing, but Mary Makebelieve knew him at once for that great policeman who guided the traffic at the Grafton Street crossing.

10

The policeman told her wonderful things. He informed her why the Phoenix Park was called the Phoenix Park. He did not believe there was a phoenix in the Zoological Gardens, although they probably had every kind of bird in the world there. It had never struck him, now he came to think of it, to look definitely for that bird, but he would do so the next time he went into the Gardens. Perhaps the young lady would allow him (it would be a much-appreciated privilege) to escort her through the Gardens some fine day—the following day, for instance. . . . ? He rather inclined to the belief that the phoenix was extinct—that is, died out; and then, again, when he called to mind the singular habits with which this bird was credited, he conceived that it had never had a real but only a mythical existence—that is, it was a makebelieve bird, a kind of fairy tale.

He further informed Mary Makebelieve that this Park was the third largest in the world, but the most beautiful. His evidence for this statement was not only the local newspaper, whose opinion might be biased by patriotism —that is, led away from the exact truth; but in the more stable testimony of reputable English journals, such as

37

and *Tit-Bits* and *Pearson's Weekly,* he found
oritative and gratifying confirmation—that is,
reed. He cited for Mary Makebelieve's incredulity
act immensity of the Park in miles, in yards, and
res, and the number of head of cattle which could
be accommodated therein if it were to be utilised for
grazing—that is, turned into grass lands; or, if trans-
formed into tillage, the number of small farmers who
would be the proprietors of economic holdings—that is,
a recondite—that is, an abstruse and a difficult scientific
and sociological term.

Mary Makebelieve scarcely dared lift her glance to
his face. An uncontrollable shyness had taken possession
of her. Her eyes could not lift without an effort; they
fluttered vainly upwards, but before reaching any height
they flinched aside and drooped again to her lap. The
astounding thought that she was sitting beside a man
warmed and affrighted her blood so that it rushed burn-
ingly to her cheeks and went shuddering back again
coldly. Her downcast eyes were almost mesmerised by
the huge tweed-clad knees which towered like monoliths
beside her. They rose much higher than her knees did,
and extended far out more than a foot and a half
beyond her own modest stretch. Her knees slanted
gently downwards as she sat, but his jagged straitly forward, like the immovable knees of a god which she had
seen once in the Museum. On one of these great knees
an equally great hand rested. Automatically she placed
her own hand on her lap and, awe-stricken, tried to
measure the difference. Her hand was very tiny and as
white as snow; it seemed so light that the breathing of a
wind might have fluttered it. The wrist was slender and
delicate, and through its milky covering faint blue veins
glimmered. A sudden and passionate wish came to her
as she watched her wrist. She wished she had a red coral
bracelet on it, or a chain of silver beaten into flat discs,
or even two twists of little green beads. The hand that
rested on the neighbouring knee was bigger by three times

than her own, the skin on it was tanned to the colour of ripe mahogany-wood, and the heat of the day had caused great purple veins to grow in knots and ridges across the back and running in big twists down to the wrists. The specific gravity of that hand seemed tremendous; she could imagine it holding down the strong neck of a bull. It moved continually while he spoke to her, closing in a tense strong grip that changed the mahogany colour to a dull whiteness, and opening again to a ponderous, inert width.

She was ashamed that she could find nothing to say. Her vocabulary had suddenly and miserably diminished to a 'yes' and 'no', only tolerably varied by a timid 'indeed' and 'I did not know that'. Against the easy clamour of his speech she could find nothing to oppose, and ordinarily her tongue tripped and eddied and veered as easily and nonchalantly as a feather in a wind. But he did not mind silence. He interpreted it rightly as the natural homage of a girl to a policeman. He liked this homage because it helped him to feel as big as he looked, and he had every belief in his ability to conduct a polite and interesting conversation with any lady for an indefinite time.

After a while Mary Makebelieve arose and was about bidding him a timid good-bye. She wished to go away to her own little room where she could look at herself and ask herself questions. She wanted to visualise herself sitting under a tree beside a man. She knew that she could reconstruct him to the smallest detail, but feared that she might not be able to reconstruct herself. When she arose he also stood up, and fell so naturally into step beside her that there was nothing to do but to walk straight on. He still withstood the burden of conversation easily and pleasantly and very learnedly. He discussed matters of high political and social moment, explaining generously the more unusual and learned words which bristled from his vocabulary. Soon they came to a more populous part of the Park. The children ceased from their play to gaze round-eyed at the little girl and the big man; their attendants looked and giggled and envied. Under these eyes Mary Makebelieve's walk became afflicted with a sideward bias which jolted her against her companion. She was furious with herself and ashamed. She set her teeth to walk easily and straightly, but constantly the jog of his elbow on her shoulder or the swing of his hand against her blouse sent her ambling wretchedly arm's-length from him. When this had occurred half a dozen times she could have plumped down on the grass and wept loudly and without restraint. At the Park gate she stopped suddenly and, with the courage of despair, bade him good-bye. He begged courteously to be allowed to see her a little way to her home, but she would not permit it, and so he lifted his hat to her. (Through her distress she could still note in a subterranean and half-conscious fashion the fact that this was the first time a man had ever uncovered before her.) As she went away down the road she felt that his eyes were following her, and her tripping walk hurried almost to a run. She wished frantically that her dress was longer than it was—that false hem! If she could have gathered a skirt in her hand, the mere holding on to something would have given her self-possession, but she feared he was looking critically at her short skirt and immodest ankles.

He stood for a time gazing after her with a smile on his great face. He knew that she knew he was watching, and as he stood he drew his hand from his pocket and tapped and smoothed his moustache. He had a red moustache; it grew very thickly, but was cropped short and square, and its fibre was so strong that it stood out above his lip like wire. One expected it to crackle when he touched it, but it never did.

II

When Mrs Makebelieve came home that night she
seemed very tired, and complained that her work at Mrs
O'Connor's house was arduous beyond any which she
had yet engaged in. She enumerated the many rooms
that were in the house : those that were covered with
carpets, the margins whereof had to be beeswaxed; those
others, only partially covered with rugs, which had to be
entirely waxed; the upper rooms were uncarpeted and
unrugged, and had, therefore, to be scrubbed; the base-
ment, consisting of two red-flagged kitchens and a scullery, had also to be scoured out. The lady was very particular about the scouring of wainscotings and doors. The
upper part of the staircase was bare and had to be
scrubbed down, and the part down to the hall had a thin
strip of carpet on it secured by brazen rods; the margins
on either side of this carpet had to be beeswaxed and the
brass rods polished. There was a great deal of unnecessary and vexatious brass of one kind or another scattered
about the house, and as there were four children in the
family, besides Mrs O'Connor and her two sisters, the
amount of washing which had constantly to be done was
enormous and terrifying.

During their tea Mrs Makebelieve called to mind the
different ornaments which stood on the parlour mantelpiece and on the top of the piano. There was a china
shepherdess with a basket of flowers at one end of the
mantelpiece and an exact duplicate on the other. In the
centre a big clock of speckled marble was surmounted
by a little domed edifice with Corinthian pillars in front,
and this again was topped by the figure of an archer with
a bent bow—there was nothing on top of this figure
because there was not any room. Between each of these
articles there stood little framed photographs of members

41

of Mrs O'Connor's family, and behind all there was a carved looking-glass with bevelled edges having many shelves. Each shelf had a cup or a saucer or a china bowl on it. On the left-hand side of the fireplace there was a plaque whereon a young lady dressed in a sky-blue robe crossed by means of well-defined stepping-stones a thin but furious stream; the middle distance was embellished by a cow, and the horizon sustained two white lambs, a brown dog, a fountain, and a sun-dial. On the right-hand side a young gentleman clad in a crimson coat and yellow knee-breeches carried a three-cornered hat under his arm, and he also crossed a stream which seemed the exact counterpart of the other one and whose perspective was similarly complicated. There were three pictures on each wall—nine in all : three of these were pictures of ships; three were pictures of battles; two portrayed saintly but emaciated personages sitting in peculiarly disheartening wildernesses (each wilderness contained one cactus plant and a camel). One of these personages stared fixedly at a skull; the other personage looked with intense firmness away from a lady of scant charms in a white and all-too-insufficient robe : above the robe a segment of the lady's bosom was hinted at bashfully—it was probably this the personage looked firmly away from. The remaining picture showed a little girl seated in a big armchair and reading with profound culture the most massive of Bibles : she had her grandmother's mutch cap and spectacles on, and looked very sweet and solemn; a doll sat bolt upright beside her, and on the floor a kitten hunted a ball of wool with great earnestness.

All these things Mrs Makebelieve discussed to her daughter, as also of the carpet which might have been woven in Turkey or elsewhere, the sideboard that possibly was not mahogany, and the chairs and occasional tables whose legs had attained to rickets through convulsions; the curtains of cream-coloured lace which were reinforced by rep hangings and guarded shutters from

Venice, also the deer's head which stood on a shelf over the door and was probably shot by a member of the family in a dream, and the splendid silver tankards which flanked this trophy and were possibly made of tin.

Mrs Makebelieve further spoke of the personal characteristics of the householder with an asperity which was still restrained. She had a hairy chin, said Mrs Makebelieve : she had buck teeth and a solid smile, and was given to telling people who knew their business how things ought to be done. Beyond this she would not say anything—the amount of soap the lady allowed to wash out five rooms and a lengthy staircase was not as generous as one was accustomed to, but, possibly, she was well-meaning enough when one came to know her better.

Mary Makebelieve, apropos of nothing, asked her mother did she ever know a girl who got married to a policeman, and did she think that policemen were good men?

Her mother replied that policemen were greatly sought after as husbands for several reasons—firstly, they were big men, and big men are always good to look upon; secondly, their social standing was very high and their respectability undoubted; thirdly, a policeman's pay was such as would bring comfort to any household which was not needlessly and criminally extravagant, and this was often supplemented in a variety of ways which rumour only hinted at (there was also the safe prospect of a pension and the possibility of a sergeantship, where the emoluments were very great); and fourthly, a policeman, being subjected for many years to a rigorous discipline, would likely make a nice and obedient husband. Personally Mrs Makebelieve did not admire policemen— they thought too much of themselves, and their continual pursuit of and intercourse with criminals tended to deteriorate their moral tone; also, being much admired by a certain type of woman, their morals were subjected to so continuous an assault that the wife of such a one would be worn to a shadow in striving to

43

preserve her husband from designing and persistent females.

Mary Makebelieve said she thought it would be nice to have other women dying for love of one's husband, but her mother opposed this with the reflection that such people did not die for love at all—they were merely anxious to gratify a foolish and excessive pride, or to inflict pain on respectable married women. On the whole, a policeman was not an ideal person to marry. The hours at which he came home were liable to constant and vexatious changes, so that there was a continual feeling of insecurity, which was bad for housekeeping; and if one had not stability in one's home all discipline and all real home life was at an end. There was this to be said for them—that they all loved little children. But, all things considered, a clerk made a better husband : his hours were regular, and knowing where he was at any moment, one's mind was at ease.

Mary Makebelieve was burning to tell some one of her adventure during the day, but although she had never before kept a secret from her mother she was unable to tell her this one. Something—perhaps the mere difference of age, and also a kind of shyness—kept her silent. She wished she knew a nice girl of her own age, or even a little younger, to whose enraptured ear she might have confided her story. They would have hugged each other during the recital, and she would have been able to enlarge upon a hundred trivialities of moustache and hair and eyes, the wonder of which older minds can seldom appreciate.

Her mother said she did not feel at all well. She did not know what was the matter with her, but she was more tired than she could remember being for a long time. There was a dull aching in all her bones, a coldness in her limbs, and when she pressed her hair backwards it hurt her head; so she went to bed much earlier than was usual. But long after her regular time for sleep had passed Mary Makebelieve crouched on the floor before the few warm coals. She was looking into the redness, seeing visions of rapture, strange things which could not possibly be true; but these visions warmed her blood and lifted her heart on light and tremulous wings; there was a singing in her ears to which she could never be tired listening.

12

Mrs Makebelieve felt much better the next morning after the extra sleep which she had. She still confessed to a slight pain in her scalp when she brushed her hair, and was a little languid, but not so much as to call for complaint. She sat up in bed while her daughter prepared the breakfast, and her tongue sped as rapidly as heretofore. She said she had a sort of feeling that her brother Patrick must come back from America some time, and she was sure that when he did return he would lose no time in finding out his relatives and sharing with them the wealth which he had amassed in that rich country. She had memories of his generosity even as a mere infant, when he would always say 'no' if only half a potato remained in the dish or a solitary slice of bread was on the platter. She delighted to talk of his good looks and high spirits and of the amazingly funny things he had said and done. There was always, of course, the chance that Patrick had got married and settled down in America, and, if so, that would account for so prolonged a silence. Wives always came between a man and his friends, and this woman would do all she could to prevent Patrick benefiting his own sister and her child. Even in Ireland there were people like that, and the more one heard of America the less one knew what to expect from strange people who were native to that place. She had often thought she would like to go out there herself, and, indeed, if she had a little money she would think nothing of packing up her things tomorrow and setting out for the States. There were fine livings to be made there, and women were greatly in request, both as servants and wives. It was well known, too, that the Americans loved Irish people, and so there would be no difficulty at all in getting a start. The more she thought of Mrs O'Connor, the more favourably she pondered on emigration. She would say nothing against Mrs O'Connor yet, but the fact remained that she had a wen on her cheek and buck teeth. Either of these afflictions taken separately was excusable, but together she fancied they betokened a bad, sour nature; but maybe the woman was to be pitied : she might be a nice person in herself, but, then, there was the matter of the soap, and she was very fond of giving unnecessary orders. However, time would show, and, clients being as scarce as they were, one could not quarrel with one's bread and butter.

The opening of a door and the stamping downstairs of heavy feet shot Mrs Makebelieve from her bed and into her clothing with furious speed. Within five minutes she was dressed, and after kissing her daughter three times she fled down the stairs and away to her business.

Mary had obtained her mother's consent to do as she pleased with the piece of black velvet on the hem of her Sunday skirt, so she passed some time in ripping this off and cleaning it. It would not come as fresh as she desired, and there were some parts of it frayed and rubbed so that the velvet was nearly lost, but other portions were quite good, and by cutting out the worn parts and neatly joining the good pieces she at last evolved a quite passable sash. Having the sash ready, she dressed herself to see how it looked, and was delighted. Then, becoming dissatisfied with the severe method of doing her hair, she manipulated it gently for a few minutes until a curl depended by both ears and two or three very tiny ones fluttered above her forehead. She put on her hat and stole out, walking very gently

46

for fear any of the other people in the house would peep through their doors as she went by. Walk as gently as she could, these bare, solid stairs rang loudly to each footfall, and so she ended in a rush and was out and away without daring to look if she was observed. She had a sort of guilty feeling as she walked, which she tried to allay by saying very definitely that she was not doing anything wrong. She said to herself with determined candour that she would walk up to the St Stephen's Green Park and look at the ducks and the flower-beds and the eels, but when she reached the quays she blushed deeply, and turning towards the right, went rapidly in the direction of the Phoenix Park. She told herself that she was not going in there, but would merely take a walk by the river, cross at Island Bridge, and go back on the opposite side of the Liffey to the Green. But when she saw the broad sunlit road gleaming through the big gates she thought she would go for a little way up there to look at the flowers behind the railings. As she went in a great figure came from behind the newspaper kiosk outside the gates and followed Mary up the road. When she paused to look at the flowers the great figure halted also, and when she went on again it followed. Mary walked past the Gough Statue and turned away into the fields and the trees, and here the figure lengthened its stride. In the middle of the field a big shadow bobbed past her shoulder, and she walked on holding her breath and watching the shadow growing by queer forward jerks. In a moment the dull beat of feet on grass banished all thought of the shadow, and then there came a cheerful voice in her ears, and the big policeman was standing by her side. For a few moments they were stationary, making salutation and excuse and explanation, and then they walked slowly on through the sunshine. Wherever there was a bush there were flowers on it. Every tree was thronged with birds that sang shrilly and sweetly in sudden thrills and clear sustained melodies, but in the open spaces the silence was more won-

47

derful; there was no bird note to come between Mary
and that deep voice, no shadow of a tree to swallow up
their own two shadows; and the sunlight was so mildly
warm, the air was so sweet and pure, and the little wind
that hushed by from the mountains was a tender and a
peaceful wind.

13

After that day Mary Makebelieve met her new friend
frequently. Somehow, wherever she went, he was not far
away; he seemed to spring out of space—one moment
she was alone watching the people passing and the hurrying cars and the thronged and splendid shop windows,
and then a big voice was booming down to her and a
big form was pacing deliberately by her side. Twice he
took her into a restaurant and gave her lunch. She had
never been in a restaurant before, and it seemed to her
like a place in fairyland. The semi-darkness of the retired
rooms faintly coloured by tiny electric lights, the beautifully clean tables and the strange foods, the neatly
dressed waitresses with quick, deft movements and
gravely attentive faces—these things thrilled her. She
noticed that the girls in the restaurant, in spite of their
gravity and industry, observed both herself and the big
man with the minutest inspection, and she felt that they
all envied her the attentions of so superb a companion.
In the street also she found that many people looked at
them, but, listening to his constant and easy speech, she
could not give these people the attention they deserved.

When they did not go to the Park they sought the
most reserved streets or walked out to the confines of
the town and up by the river Dodder. There are exqui-
sitely beautiful places along the side of the Dodder: shy
little harbours and backwaters, and now and then a

miniature waterfall or a broad, placid reach upon which the sun beats down like silver. Along the river-bank the grass grows rank and wildly luxurious, and at this season, warmed by the sun, it was a splendid place to sit. She thought she could sit there for ever watching the shining river and listening to the great voice by her side.

He told her many things about himself and about his comrades—those equally huge men. She could see them walking with slow vigour through their barrack-yard, falling in for exercise or gymnastics or for school. She wondered what they were taught, and who had sufficient impertinence to teach giants, and were they ever slapped for not knowing their lessons? He told her of his daily work, the hours when he was on and off duty, the hours when he rose in the morning and when he went to bed. He told her of night duty, and drew a picture of the blank deserted streets which thrilled and frightened her . . . the tense darkness, and how through the silence the sound of a footstep was magnified a thousand-fold, ringing down the desolate pathways away and away to the smallest shrill distinctness; and she saw also the alleys and lane-ways hooded in blackness, and the one or two human fragments who drifted aimless and frantic along the lonely streets, striving to walk easily for fear of their own thundering footsteps, cowering in the vastness of the city, dwarfed and shivering beside the gaunt houses; the thousands upon thousands of black houses, each deadly silent, each seeming to wait and listen for the morning, and each teeming with men and women who slept in peace because he was walking up and down outside, flashing his lantern on shop windows, and feeling doors to see if they were by any chance open. Now and again a step from a great distance would tap-tap-tap, a far-off delicacy of sound, and either die away down echoing side streets or come clanking on to where he stood, growing louder and clearer and more resonant, ringing again and again in doubled and trebled echoes; while he, standing far back in a doorway, watched to see who was abroad at the dead of night—and then that person went away on his strange errand, his footsteps trampling down immense distances, till the last echo and the last faint tremble of his feet eddied into the stillness. Now and again a cat dodged gingerly along a railing, or a strayed dog slunk fearfully down the pathway, nosing everywhere in and out of the lamplight, silent and hungry and desperately eager. He told her stories also, wonderful tales of great fights and cunning tricks, of men and women whose whole lives were tricks, of people who did not know how to live except by theft and violence; people who were born by stealth, who ate by subterfuge, drank by dodges, got married in attics, and slid into death by strange, subterranean passages. He told her the story of the Two Hungry Men, and of The Sailor who had been Robbed, and a funny tale about The Barber who had Two Mothers. He also told her the stories of The Eight Tinkers and of The Old Women who Steal Fish at Night-time, and the story of The Men he Let Off, and he told her a terrible story of how he fought five men in a little room, and he showed her a great livid scar hidden by his cap, and the marks in his neck where he had been stabbed with a jagged bottle, and his wrists which an Italian madman had thrust through and through with a dagger.

But though he was always talking, he was not always talking of himself. Through his conversation there ran a succession of queries—tiny, slender questions which ran out of his stories and into her life—questions so skilful and natural and spontaneous that only a girl could discover the curiosity which prompted them. He wanted her name, her address, her mother's name, her father's name; had she other relatives, did she go to work yet, what was her religion, was it a long time since she left school, and what was her mother's business? To all of these Mary Makebelieve answered with glad candour. She saw each question coming, and the personal curiosity lying behind it she divined and was glad of. She would have loved to ask him personal and intimate questions about his parents, his brothers and sisters, and what he said when he said his prayers, and had he walked with other girls, and, if so, what had he said to them, and what did he really and truly think of her? Her curiosity on all these points was abundant and eager, but she did not dare to even hint a question.

One of the queries often touched upon by him she eluded—she shrank from it with something like terror— it was, 'What was her mother's business?' She could not bear to say that her mother was a charwoman. It did not seem fitting. She suddenly hated and was ashamed of this occupation. It took on an aspect of incredible baseness. It seemed to be the meanest employment wherein any one could be engaged; and so when the question, conveyed in a variety of ways, had to be answered it was answered with reservations—Mary Makebelieve told him a lie. She said her mother was a dressmaker.

14

One night when Mrs Makebelieve came home she was very low-spirited indeed. She complained once more of a headache and of a languor which she could not account for. She said it gave her all the trouble in the world to lift a bucket. It was not exactly that she could not lift a bucket, but that she could scarcely close her mind down to the fact that a bucket had to be lifted. Some spring of willingness seemed to be temporarily absent. To close her two hands on a floor-cloth and twist it into a spiral in order to wring it thoroughly was a thing which she found herself imagining she could do if she liked, but had not the least wish to do. These duties, even when she was engaged in them, had a curious quality of remoteness. The bucket into which her

51

hand had been plunged a moment before seemed somehow incredibly distant. To lift the soap lying beside the bucket one would require an arm of more than human reach, and having washed, or rather dabbed, at a square of flooring, it was a matter of grave concern how to reach the unwashed part just beyond without moving herself. This languor alarmed her. The pain in her head, while it was severe, did not really matter. Everyone had pains and aches, sores and sprains, but this unknown weariness and disinclination for the very slightest exertion gave her a fright.

Mary tempted her to come out and watch the people going into the Gaiety Theatre. She said a certain actor was playing whom all the women of Dublin make pilgrimages, even from distant places, to look at; and by going at once they might be in time to see him arriving in a motor-car at the stage door, when they could have a good look at him getting out of the car and going into the theatre. At these tidings Mrs Makebelieve roused for a moment from her strange apathy. Since tea-time she had sat (not as usual upright and gesticulating, but humped up and flaccid) staring at a blob of condensed milk on the outside of the tin. She said she thought she would go out and see the great actor, although what all the women saw in him to go mad about she did not know, but in another moment she settled back to her humped-up position and restored her gaze to the condensed milk tin. With a little trouble Mary got her to bed, where, after being hugged for one moment, she went swiftly and soundly to sleep.

Mary was troubled because of her mother's illness, but, as it is always difficult to believe in the serious illness of another person until death has demonstrated its gravity, she soon dismissed the matter from her mind. This was the more easily done because her mind was teeming with impressions and pictures and scraps of dialogue.

As her mother was sleeping peacefully, Mary put on

her hat and went out. She wanted, in her then state of mind, to walk in the solitude which can only be found in crowded places, and also she wanted some kind of distraction. Her days had lately been so filled with adventure that the placid immobility of the top back room was not only irksome but maddening, and her mother's hasty and troubled breathing came between her and her thoughts. The poor furniture of the room was hideous to her eyes; the uncarpeted floor and bleak, stained walls dulled her.

She went out, and in a few moments was part of the crowd which passes and repasses nightly from the Rotunda up the broad pathways of Sackville Street, across O'Connell Bridge, up Westmoreland Street, past Trinity College, and on through the brilliant lights of Grafton Street to the Fusiliers' Arch at the entrance to St Stephen's Green Park. Here from half-past seven o'clock in the evening youthful Dublin marches in joyous procession. Sometimes bevies of young girls dance by, each a giggle incarnate. A little distance behind these a troop of young men follow stealthily and critically. They will be acquainted and more or less happily paired before the Bridge is reached. But generally the movement is in couples. Appointments, dating from the previous night, have filled the streets with happy and careless boys and girls—they are not exactly courting, they are enjoying the excitement of fresh acquaintance; old conversation is here poured into new bottles, old jokes have the freshn ss of infancy; every one is animated, and polite to no one but his partner; the people they meet and pass and those who overtake and pass them are all subjects for their wit and scorn, while they, in turn, furnish a moment's amusement and conversation to each succeeding couple. Constantly there are stoppages when very high-bred introductions result in a redistribution of the youngsters. As they move apart the words 'Tomorrow night', or 'Thursday', or 'Friday' are called laughingly back, showing that the late partner is not to be lost sight of utterly; and then the procession begins anew.

Among these folk Mary Makebelieve passed rapidly. She knew that if she walked slowly some partially-elaborate gentleman would ask suddenly what she had been doing with herself since last Thursday, and would introduce her as Kate Ellen to six precisely similar young gentlemen, who smiled blandly in a semicircle six feet distant. This had happened to her once before, and as she fled the six young gentlemen had roared 'Bow, wow, wow' after her, while the seventh mewed earnestly and with noise.

She stood for a time watching the people thronging into the Gaiety Theatre. Some came in motor-cabs, others in carriages. Many hearse-like cabs deposited weighty and respectable solemnities under the glass-roofed vestibule. Swift outside cars buzzed on rubber tyres with gentlemen clad in evening dress, and ladies whose silken wraps blew gently from their shoulders, and, in addition, a constant pedestrian stream surged along the pathway. From the shelter of an opposite doorway Mary watched these gaily animated people. She envied them all innocently enough, and wondered would the big policeman ever ask her to go to the theatre with him, and if he did, would her mother let her go. She thought her mother would refuse, but was dimly certain that in some way she would manage to get out if such a delightful invitation were given her. She was dreaming of the alterations she would make in her best frock in anticipation of such a treat when, half-consciously, she saw a big figure appear round the corner of Grafton Street and walk towards the theatre. It was he, and her heart jumped with delight. She prayed that he would not see her, and then she prayed that he would, and then, with a sudden, sickening coldness, she saw that he was not alone. A young, plump, rosy-cheeked girl was at his side. As they came nearer the girl put her arm into his and said something. He bent down to her and replied, and she flashed a laugh up at him. There was a swift

54

interchange of sentences, and they both laughed together; then they disappeared into the half-crown door.

Mary shrank back into the shadow of the doorway. She had a strange notion that everybody was trying to look at her, and that they were all laughing maliciously. After a few moments she stepped out on the path and walked homewards quickly. She did not hear the noises of the streets, nor see the promenading crowds. Her face was bent down as she walked, and beneath the big brim of her straw hat her eyes were blinded with the bitterest tears she had ever shed.

15

Next morning her mother was no better. She made no attempt to get out of bed, and listened with absolute indifference when the morning feet of the next-door man pounded the stairs. Mary awakened her again and again, but each time, after saying 'All right, dearie,' she relapsed to a slumber which was more torpor than sleep. Her yellow, old-ivory face was faintly tinged with colour; her thin lips were relaxed, and seemed a trifle fuller, so that Mary thought she looked better in sickness than in health; but the limp arm lying on the patchwork quilt seemed to be more skinny than thin, and the hand was more waxen and claw-like than heretofore.

Mary laid the breakfast on the bed as usual, and again awakened her mother, who, after staring into vacancy for a few moments, forced herself to her elbow, and then, with sudden determination, sat up in the bed and bent her mind inflexibly on her breakfast. She drank two cups of tea greedily, but the bread had no taste in her mouth, and after swallowing a morsel she laid it aside.

'I don't know what's up with me at all, at all,' said she.

'Maybe it's a cold, mother,' replied Mary.

'Do I look bad, now?'

Mary scrutinised her narrowly.

'No,' she answered; 'your face is redder than it does be, and your eyes are shiny. I think you look splendid and well. What way do you feel?'

'I don't feel at all, except that I'm sleepy. Give me the glass in my hand, dearie, till I see what I'm like.'

Mary took the glass from the wall and handed it to her.

'I don't look bad at all. A bit of colour always suited me. Look at my tongue though, it's very, very dirty; it's a bad tongue altogether. My mother had a tongue like that, Mary, when she died.'

'Have you any pain?' said her daughter.

'No, dearie; there is a buzz in the front of my head as if something was spinning round and round very quickly, and that makes my eyes tired, and there's a sort of feeling as if my head was twice as heavy as it should be. Hang up the glass again. I'll try and get a sleep, and maybe I'll be better when I waken up. Run you out and get a bit of steak, and we'll stew it down and make beef-tea, and maybe that will do me good. Give me my purse out of the pocket of my skirt.'

Mary found the purse and brought it to the bed. Her mother opened it and brought out a thimble, a bootlace, five buttons, one sixpenny piece and a penny. She gave Mary the sixpence.

'Get half a pound of leg beef,' said she, 'and then we'll have fourpence left for bread and tea : no, take the other penny, too, and get half a pound of pieces at the butcher's for twopence, and a twopenny tin of condensed milk, that's fourpence; and a three-ha'penny loaf and one penny for tea, that's sixpence ha'penny; and get onions with the odd ha'penny, and we'll put them in the beef-tea. Don't forget, dearie, to pick lean bits of meat; them fellows do be always trying to stick bits of bone and gristle on a body. Tell him it's for beef-tea for your mother, and that I'm not well at all, and ask how Mrs

Quinn is; she hasn't been down in the shop for a long time. I'll go to sleep now. I'll have to go to work in the morning whatever happens, because there isn't any money in the house at all. Come home as quick as you can, dearie.'

Mary dressed herself and went out for the provisions, but she did not buy them at once. As she went down the street she turned suddenly, clasping her hands in a desperate movement, and walked very quickly in the opposite direction. She turned up the side streets to the quays, and along these to the Park gates. Her hands were clasping and unclasping in an agony of impatience, and her eyes roved busily here and there, flying among the few pedestrians like lanterns. She went through the gates and up the broad central path, and here she walked more slowly : but she did not see the flowers behind the railings, or even the sunshine that bathed the world in glory. At the monument she sped a furtive glance down the road she had travelled—there was nobody behind her. She turned into the fields, walking under trees which she did not see. and up hills and down valleys without noticing the incline of either. At times, through the tatter of her mind there blazed a memory of her mother lying sick at home, waiting for her daughter to return with food, and at such memories she gripped her hands together frightfully and banished the thought. A moment's reflection and she could have hated her mother.

It was nearly five o'clock before she left the Park. She walked in a fog of depression. For hours she had gone hither and thither in the well-remembered circle, every step becoming more wayward and aimless. The sun had disappeared, and a grey evening bowed down upon the fields; the little wind that whispered along the grass or swung the light branches of the trees had a bleak edge to it. As she left the big gates she was chilled through and through, but the memory of her mother now set her running homewards. For the time she forgot her quest among the trees, and thought only, with shame and fear, of what her mother would say, and of the reproachful, amazed eyes which would be turned on her when she went in. What could she say? She could not imagine anything. How could she justify a neglect which must appear gratuitous, cold-blooded, inexplicable?

When she had brought the food and climbed the resonant stairs she stood outside the door crying softly to herself. She hated to open the door. She could imagine her mother sitting up in the bed dazed and unbelieving, angry and frightened, imagining accidents and terrors, and when she would go in. . . . She had an impulse to open the door gently, leave the food just inside, and run down the stairs out into the world anywhere and never come back again. At last in desperation she turned the handle and stepped inside. Her face flamed; the blood burned her eyes physically so that she could not see through them. She did not look at the bed, but went direct to the fireplace, and with a dogged patience began mending the fire. After a few stubborn moments she twisted violently to face whatever might come, ready to break into angry reproaches and impertinences; but her mother was lying very still. She was fast asleep, and a weight, an absolutely real pressure, was lifted from Mary's heart. Her fingers flew about the preparation of the beef-tea. She forgot the man whom she had gone to meet. Her arms were tired and hungry to close around her mother. She wanted to whisper little childish words to her, to rock her to and fro on her breast, and croon little songs and kiss her and pat her face.

16

Her mother did not get better. Indeed, she got worse. In addition to the lassitude of which she had complained, she suffered also from great heat and great cold, and, furthermore, sharp pains darted so swiftly through her brows that at times she was both dizzy and sightless. A twirling movement in her head prevented her from standing up. Her centre of gravity seemed destroyed, for when she did stand and attempted to walk she had a strange bearing away on one side, so that on striving to walk towards the door she veered irresistibly at least four feet to the left-hand side of that point. Mary Makebelieve helped her back to bed, where she lay for a time watching horizontal lines spinning violently in front of her face, and these lines after a time crossed and recrossed each other in so mazy and intricate a pattern that she became violently sick from the mere looking at them.

All of these things she described to her daughter, tracing the queer patterns which were spinning about her with such fidelity that Mary was almost able to see them. She also theorised about the cause and ultimate effect of these symptoms, and explained the degrees of heat and cold which burned or chilled her, and the growth of a pain to its exquisite startling apex, its subsequent slow recession, and the thud of an india-rubber hammer which ensued when the pain had ebbed to its easiest level. It did not occur to either of them to send for a doctor. Doctors in such cases are seldom sent for, seldom even thought of One falls sick according to some severely definite, implacable law with which it is foolish to quarrel, and one gets well again for no other reason than that it is impossible to be sick for ever. As the night struggles slowly into day, so sickness climbs stealthily into health, and nature has a system of medicining her ailments which might only be thwarted by the ministrations of a mere doctor. Doctors also expect payment for their services—an expectation so wildly beyond the range of common sense as to be ludicrous. Those who can scarcely fee a baker when they are in health can certainly not remunerate a physician when they are ill.

But, despite her sickness, Mrs Makebelieve was worried with the practical common politics of existence. The food purchased with her last sevenpence was eaten beyond remembrance. The vital requirements of the next day, and the following day, and of all subsequent days thronged upon her, clamouring for instant attention. The wraith of a landlord sat on her bed demanding rent and threatening grisly alternatives. Goblins that were bakers and butchers and grocers grinned and leered and jabbered from the corners of the room.

Each day Mary Makebelieve went to the pawn office with something. They lived for a time on the only capital they had—the poor furniture of their room. Everything which had even the narrowest margin of value was sold. Mary's dresses kept them for six days. Her mother's Sunday skirt fed them for another day. They held famine at bay with a patchwork quilt and a crazy wash-stand. A water-jug and a strip of oilcloth tinkled momentarily against the teeth of the wolf and disappeared. The maw of hunger was not incommoded by the window curtain.

At last the room was as bare as a desert and almost as uninhabitable. A room without furniture is a ghostly place. Sounds made therein are uncanny; even the voice puts off its humanity and rings back with a bleak and hollow note, an empty resonance tinged with the frost of winter. There is no other sound so deadly, so barren and dispiriting, as the echoes of an empty room. The gaunt woman in the bed seemed less gaunt than her residence, and there was nothing more to be sent to the pawnbroker or the second-hand dealer.

A postcard came from Mrs O'Connor requesting, in the peremptory language customary to such communications, that Mrs Makebelieve would please call on her the following morning before eight o'clock. Mrs Makebelieve groaned as she read it. It meant work and food and the repurchase of her household goods, and she knew that on the following morning she would not be able to get up. She lay a while thinking, and then called her daughter.

'Dearie,' said she, 'you will have to go to this place in the morning and try what you can do. Tell Mrs O'Connor that I am sick, and that you are my daughter and will do the work, and try and do the best you can for a while.'

She caught her daughter's head down to her bosom and wept over her, for she saw in this work a beginning and an end—the end of the little daughter who could be petted and rocked and advised; the beginning of a womanhood which would grow up to and beyond her, which would collect and secrete emotions and aspirations and adventures not to be shared even by a mother; and she saw the failure which this work meant, the expanding of her daughter's life ripples to a bleak and miserable horizon where the clouds were soap-suds and floor-cloths, and the beyond a blank resignation only made energetic by hunger.

'Oh, my dear,' said she, 'I hate to think of you having to do such work, but it will only be for a while, a week, and then I will be well again. Only a little week, my love, my sweetheart, my heart's darling.'

17

Early on the following morning Mary Makebelieve awakened with a start. She felt as if some one had called her, and lay for a few moments to see had her mother spoken. But her mother was still asleep. Her slumber was at all times almost as energetic as her wakening hours. She twisted constantly and moved her hands and spoke ramblingly. Odd interjections, such as 'Ah, well!' 'No matter!' 'Certainly not!' and 'Indeed aye!' shot from her lips like bullets, and at intervals a sarcastic sniff fretted or astonished her bedfellow into wakefulness. But now as she lay none of these strenuous ejaculations were audible. Sighs only, weighty and deep-drawn and very tired, broke on her lips and lapsed sadly into the desolate room.

Mary Makebelieve lay for a time wondering idly what had awakened her so completely, for her eyes were wide open and every vestige of sleep was gone from her brain; and then she remembered that on this morning, and for the first time in her life, she had to go to work. That knowledge had gone to bed with her and had awakened her with an imperious urgency. In an instant she sprang out of bed, huddled on sufficient clothing for warmth, and set about lighting the fire. She was far too early awake, but could not compose herself to lie for another moment in bed. She did not at all welcome the idea of going to work, but the interest attaching to a new thing, the freshness which vitalises for a time even the dreariest undertaking, prevented her from rueing with any bitterness her first day's work. To a young person even work is an adventure, and anything which changes the usual current of life is welcome. The fire also went with her; in quite a short time the flames had gathered to a blaze, and matured, and concentrated to the glowing redness of perfect combustion; then, when the smoke had disappeared with the flames, she put on the saucepan of water. Quickly the saucepan boiled, and she wet the tea. She cut the bread into slices, put a spoonful of condensed milk into each cup, and awakened her mother.

All through the breakfast her mother advised her on the doing of her work. She cautioned her daughter when scrubbing woodwork always to scrub against the grain, for this gave a greater purchase to the brush, and removed the dirt twice as quickly as the seemingly easy opposite movement. She told her never to save soap—little soap meant much rubbing—and advised that she should scrub two minutes with one hand and then two minutes with the other hand; and she was urgent on the necessity of thoroughness in the wringing out of one's floor-cloth, because a dry floor-cloth takes up twice as much water as a wet one, and thus lightens labour; also she advised Mary to change her positions as frequently as possible to avoid cramp when scrubbing, and to kneel up or stand up when wringing her cloths, as this would give her a rest, and the change of movement would relieve her very greatly; and above all to take her time about the business, because haste seldom resulted in clean work, and was never appreciated by one's employer.

Before going out Mary Makebelieve had to arrange for some one to look after her mother during the day. This is an arrangement which, among poor people, is never difficult of accomplishment. The first to whom she applied was the labouring man's wife in the next room; she was a vast woman with six children and a laugh like the rolling of a great wind, and when Mary Makebelieve advanced her request she shook six children off her like toys and came out on the landing.

'Run off to your work now, honey,' said she, 'and let you be easy in your mind about your mother, for I'll go up to her this minute, and when I'm not there myself I'll leave one of the children with her to call me if she wants anything; and don't you be fretting at all, God help you! for she'll be as safe and as comfortable with me as if she was in Jervis Street Hospital or the Rotunda itself. What's wrong with her now? Is it a pain in her head she has, or a sick stomach, God help her?'

Mary explained briefly, and as she went down the stairs she saw the big woman going into her mother's room.

She had not been out in the streets so early before, and had never known the wonder and beauty of the sun in the early morning. The streets were almost deserted, and the sunlight—a most delicate and nearly colourless radiance—fell gently on the long silent paths. Missing the customary throng of people and traffic, she seemed almost in a strange country, and had to look twice for turnings which she could easily have found with her eyes shut. The shutters were up in all the shops, and the blinds were down in most of the windows. Now and again a milk cart came clattering and rattling down a street, and now and again a big red-painted baker's cart dashed along the road. Such few pedestrians as she met were poorly dressed men, who carried tommy cans and tools, and they were all walking at a great pace, as if they feared they were late for somewhere. Three or four boys passed her running; one of these had a great lump of bread in his hand, and as he ran he tore pieces off the bread with his teeth and ate them. The streets looked cleaner than she had thought they could look, and the houses seemed very quiet and beautiful. When she came near a policeman she looked at him keenly from a distance, hoping and fearing that it might be her friend, but she did not see him. She had a sinking feeling at the thought that maybe he would be in the Phoenix Park this day looking for her, and might, indeed, have been there for the past few days, and the thought that he might be seeking for her unavailingly stabbed through her mind like a pain. It did not seem right, it was not in proportion, that so big a man should seek for a mere woman and not find one instantly to hand. It was pitiful to think of the huge man looking on this side and on that, peering behind trees and through distances, and thinking that maybe he was forgotten or scorned. Mary Makebelieve almost wept at the idea that he should fancy she scorned him. She wondered how, under such circumstances, a small girl can comfort a big man. One may fondle his hand, but that is miserably inadequate. She wished she was twice as big as he was, so that she might lift him bodily to her breast and snuggle and hug him like a kitten. So comprehensive an embrace alone could atone for injury to a big man's feelings.

In about twenty minutes she reached Mrs O'Connor's house and knocked. She had to knock half a dozen times before she was admitted, and on being admitted had a great deal of trouble explaining who she was, and why

64

her mother had not come, and that she was quite competent to undertake the work. She knew the person who opened the door for her was not Mrs O'Connor, because she had not a hairy wart on her chin, nor had she buck teeth. After a little delay she was brought to the scullery and given a great pile of children's clothing to wash, and after starting this work she was left to herself for a long time.

18

It was a dark house. The windows were all withered away behind stiff curtains, and the light that laboured between these was chastened to the last degree of respectability. The doors skulked behind heavy plush hangings. The floors hid themselves decently under thick red and black carpets, and the margins which were uncarpeted were disguised by beeswax, so that no one knew they were there at all. The narrow hall was steeped in shadow, for there two black velvet portières, at distances of six feet apart, depended from rods in the ceiling. Similar palls flopped on each landing of the staircase, and no sound was heard in the house at all, except dim voices that droned from somewhere, muffled and sepulchral and bodiless.

At ten o'clock, having finished the washing, Mary was visited by Mrs O'Connor, whom she knew at once by the signs she had been warned of. The lady subjected each article that had been washed to a particular scrutiny, and, with the shadowy gallop of a smile that dashed into and out of sight in an instant, said they would do. She then conducted Mary to the kitchen and, pointing to a cup of tea and two slices of bread, invited her to breakfast, and left her for six minutes, when she reappeared with the suddenness of a marionette and directed her to wash her cup and saucer, and then to wash the kitchen, and these things also Mary did.

She got weary very soon, but not dispirited, because there were many things to look at in the kitchen. There were pots of various sizes and metals, saucepans little and big, jugs of all shapes, and a regiment of tea things were ranged on the dresser; on the walls were hung great pot-lids like the shields of barbarous warriors which she had seen in a story-book. Under the kitchen table there was a row of boots, all wrinkled by usage, and each wearing a human and almost intelligent aspect—a well-wrinkled boot has often an appearance of mad humanity which can chain and almost hypnotise the observer. As she lifted the boots out of her way she named each by its face. There was Grubtoes, Sloucher, Thump-thump, Hoppit, Twitter, Hide-away, and Fairybell.

While she was working a young girl came into the kitchen and took up the boots called Fairybell. Mary just tossed a look at her as she entered and bent again to her washing. Then with an extreme perturbation she stole another look. The girl was young and as trim as a sunny garden. Her face was packed with laughter and freedom, like a young morning when tender rosy clouds sail in the sky. She walked with a light spring of happiness; each step seemed the beginning of a dance, light and swift and certain. Mary knew her in a pang, and her bent face grew redder than the tiles she was scrubbing. Like lightning she knew her. Her brain swung in a clamour of 'Where, where?' and even in the question she had the answer, for this was the girl she had seen going into the Gaiety Theatre swinging on the arm of her big policeman. The girl said 'Good morning' to her in a kindly voice, and Mary, with a swift, frightened glance, whispered back 'Good morning'; then the girl went upstairs again, and Mary continued to scrub the floor.

When the kitchen was finished and inspected and approved of, she was instructed to wash out the front hall, and set about the work at once.

'Get it done as quickly as you can,' said the mistress; 'I am expecting my nephew here soon, and he dislikes washing.'

So Mary bent quickly to her work. She was not tired now. Her hands moved swiftly up and down the floor without effort. Indeed, her actions were almost mechanical. The self that was thinking and probing seemed somehow apart from the body bending over the bucket, and the hands that scrubbed and dipped and wrung. She had finished about three-quarters of the hall when a couple of sharp raps came to the door. Mrs O'Connor flew noiselessly up from the kitchen.

'I knew,' said she bitterly, 'that you would not be finished before he came. Dry that puddle at once, so that he can walk in, and take the soap out of the way.'

She stood with her hand on the door while Mary followed these directions; then, when a couple of hasty movements had removed the surplus water, Mrs O'Connor drew the bolt and her nephew entered. Mary knew him on the doorstep, and her blood froze in terror and boiled again in shame.

Mrs O'Connor drew the big policeman inside and kissed him.

'I can't get these people to do things in time,' said she. 'They are that slow! Hang up your hat and coat and come into the parlour.'

The policeman, with his eyes fixed steadily on Mary, began to take off his coat. His eyes, his moustache, all his face and figure seemed to be looking at her. He was an enormous and terrifying interrogation. He tapped his tough moustache and stepped over the bucket; at the entrance to the parlour he stood again and hung his monstrous look on her. He seemed about to speak, but it was to Mrs O'Connor his words went.

'How's everything?' said he; and then the door closed behind him.

Mary, with extraordinary slowness, knelt down again beside the bucket and began to scrub. She worked very deliberately, sometimes cleaning the same place two or three times. Now and again she sighed, but without any consciousness of trouble. These were sighs which did not seem to belong to her. She knew she was sighing, but could not exactly see how the dull sounds came from her lips when she had no desire to sigh and did not make any conscious effort to do so. Her mind was an absolute blank; she could think of nothing but the bubbles which broke on the floor and in the bucket, and the way the water squeezed down from the cloth. There was something she could have thought about if she wanted to, but she did not want to.

Mrs O'Connor came out in a few minutes, inspected the hall, and said it would do. She paid Mary her wages and told her to come again the next day, and Mary went home. As she walked along she was very careful not to step on any of the lines on the pavement; she walked between these, and was distressed because these lines were not equally distant from each other, so that she had to make unequal paces as she went.

19

The name of the woman from next door was Mrs Cafferty. She was big and round, and when she walked her dress whirled about her like a tempest. She seemed to be always turning round; when she was going straight forward in any direction, say towards a press, she would turn aside midway so sharply that her clothing spun gustily in her wake—this probably came from having many children. A mother is continually driving in oblique directions from her household employments to rescue her children from a mulitude of perils. An infant and a fireplace act upon each other like magnets; a small boy is always trying to eat a kettle or a piece of coal or the backbone of a herring; a little girl and a slop-bucket are in immediate contact; the baby has a knife in its mouth, the twin is on the point of swallowing a marble, or is trying to wash itself in the butter, or the cat is about to take a nap on its face. Indeed, the woman who has six children never knows in what direction her next step must be, and the continual strain of preserving her progeny converts many a one into regular cyclones of eyes and arms and legs. It also induces in some a perpetual good-humoured irritability wherein one can slap and cuddle a child in the same instant, or shout threateningly or lovingly, call warningly and murmur encouragingly in an astonishing sequence. The woman with six children must both physically and mentally travel at a tangent, and when a husband has to be badgered or humoured into the bargain, then the life of such a woman is more complex than is readily understood.

When Mary came home Mrs Cafferty was sitting on her mother's bed, two small children and a cat were also on the bed, two slightly bigger children were under the bed, and two others were galloping furiously up and down the room. At one moment these latter twain were runaway horses, at another they were express trains. When they were horses they snorted and neighed and kicked; when they were trains they backed and shunted, blew whistles and blew off steam. The children under the bed were tigers in a jungle, and they made the noises proper to such beasts and such a place; they bit each other furiously, and howled and growled precisely as tigers do. The pair of infants on the bed were playing the game of bump; they would stand upright, then spring high into the air, and come crashing down on the bed, which then sprung them partly up again. Each time they jumped they screamed loudly, each time they fell they roared delighted congratulations to each other, and when they fell together they fought with strong good humour. Sometimes they fell on Mrs Makebelieve, always they bumped her. At the side of the bed their mother sat telling with a gigantic voice a story wherein her husband's sister figured as the despicable person she was to the eye of discernment, and this story was punctuated and shot through and dislocuted by objurgations, threats, pleadings, admirations, alarms, and despairs addressed to the children separately and *en masse*, by name, nickname, and hastily created epithet.

Mary halted in amazement in the doorway. She could not grasp all the pandemonium at once, and while she stood Mrs Cafferty saw her.

'Come on in, honey,' said she. 'Your ma's as right as a trivet. All she wanted was a bit of good company and some children to play with. Deed,' she continued, 'children are the best medicine for a woman that I know of. They don't give you time to be sick, the creatures!— Patrick John, I'll give you a smack on the side of the head if you don't let your little sister alone; and don't you, Norah, be vexing him or you'll deserve all you get. Run inside, Julia Elizabeth, cut a slice of bread for the twins, and put a bit of sugar on it, honey. Yes, alanna, you can have a slice for yourself, too, you poor child you, well you deserve it.'

Mrs Makebelieve was sitting up in the bed with two pillows propping up her back. One of her long thin arms was stretched out to preserve the twins from being bruised against the wall in their play. Plainly they had become great friends with her, for every now and then they swarmed over her, and a hugging match of extreme complexity ensued. She looked almost her usual self, and all the animation which had been so marked a feature of her personality had returned to her.

'Are you better, mother?' said Mary.

Mrs Makebelieve took her daughter's head in her hands and kissed her until the twins butted them apart, clamouring for caresses.

'I am, honey,' said she. 'Those children done me good. I could have got up at one o'clock, I felt so well, but Mrs Cafferty thought I'd better not.'

'I did so,' said Mrs Cafferty. ' "Not a foot do you stir out of that bed till your daughter comes home, ma'am," said I. For do you see, child, many's the time you'd be thinking you were well and feeling as fit as a fiddle, and nothing would be doing you but to be up and gallivanting about, and then the next day you'd have a relapse, and the next day you'd be twice as bad, and the day after that they'd be measuring you for your coffin maybe. I knew a woman was taken like that—up she got; "I'm as well as ever I was," said she, and she ate a feed of pig's cheek and cabbage and finished her washing, and they buried her in a week. It's the quare thing sickness. What I say, when you're sick get into bed and stop there.'

'It's easy saying that,' said Mrs Makebelieve.

'Sure, don't I know, you poor thing you,' said Mrs Cafferty; 'but you should stay in bed as long as you are able to, anyhow.'

'How did you get on with Mrs O'Connor?' said Mrs Makebelieve.

'That's the mistress, isn't it?' queried Mrs Cafferty; 'an ould devil, I'll bet you.'

Mrs Makebelieve rapidly and lightly sketched Mrs O'Connor's leading peculiarities.

'It's queer the people one has to work for, God knows it is,' said Mrs Cafferty.

At this point a grave controversy on work might have arisen, but the children, caring little for conversation, broke into so tumultuous play that talk could not be proceeded with. Mary was enticed into a game composed in part of pussy-four-corners and tip-and-tig, with a general flavour of leap-frog working through. In five minutes her hair and her stockings were both down, and the back of her skirt had crawled threequarters round to the front. The twins shouted and bumped on the bed, upon which and on Mrs Makebelieve they rubbed bread and butter and sugar, while their mother roared an anecdote at Mrs Makebelieve in tones that ruled the din as a fog-horn rules the waves.

20

Mary had lavished the entire of her first day's wages on delicate foods wherewith to tempt her mother's languid appetite, and when the morning dawned she arose silently, lit the fire, wet the tea, and spread her purchases out on the side of the bed. There was a slice of brawn, two pork sausages, two eggs, three rashers of bacon, a bun, a pennyworth of sweets, and a pig's foot. These with bread and butter and tea made a collection amid which an invalid might browse with some satisfaction. Mary then awakened her and sat by in a dream of happiness watching her mother's eye roll slowly and unbelievingly from item to item. Mrs Makebelieve tipped each article with her first finger and put its right name on it unerringly. Then she picked out an important-looking sweet that had four colours and shone like the sun, and put it in her mouth.

'I never saw anything like it, you good child you,' said she.

Mary rocked herself to and fro and laughed loudly for delight, and then they ate a bit of everything, and were very happy.

Mrs Makebelieve said that she felt altogether better that morning. She had slept like a top all through the night, and, moreover, had a dream wherein she saw her brother Patrick standing on the remotest sea point of distant America, from whence he had shouted loudly across the ocean that he was coming back to Ireland soon, that he had succeeded very well indeed, and that he was not married. He had not changed in the slightest degree, said Mrs Makebelieve, and he looked as young and as jolly as when he was at home with her father and herself in the County Meath twenty-two years before. This mollifying dream and the easy sleep which followed it had completely restored her health and spirits. Mrs Make-believe further intimated that she intended to go to work that day. It did not fit in with her ideas of propriety that her child should turn into a charwoman, the more particularly as there was a strong—an almost certain—possibility of an early betterment of her own and her daughter's fortunes.

Dreams, said Mrs Makebelieve, did not come for nothing. There was more in dreams than was generally understood. Many and many were the dreams which she herself had been visited by, and they had come true so often that she could no longer disregard their promises, admonishments, or threats. Of course many people had dreams which were of no consequence, and these could usually be traced to gluttony or a flighty, inconstant imagination. Drunken people, for instance, often dreamed strange and terrible things, but, even while they were awake, these people were liable to imaginary enemies whom their clouded eyes and intellects magnified beyond any thoughtful proportions, and when they were asleep their dreams would also be subject to this haze and whirl of unreality and hallucination.

Mary said that sometimes she did not dream at all, and at other times she dreamed very vividly, but usually could not remember what the dream had been about when she awakened; and once she had dreamed that some one gave her a shilling which she placed carefully under her pillow, and this dream was so real that in the morning she put her hand under the pillow to see if the shilling was there, but it was not. The very next night she dreamed the same dream, and as she put the phantom money under her pillow she said out loudly to herself, 'I am dreaming this, and I dreamt it last night also'. Her mother said if she had dreamt it for the third time some one would have given her a shilling surely. To this Mary agreed, and admitted that she had tried very hard to dream it on the third night, but somehow could not do it.

'When my brother comes home from America,' said Mrs Makebelieve, 'we'll go away from this part of the city at once. I suppose he'd want a rather big house on the south side—Rathfarnham or Terenure way, or, maybe, Donnybrook. Of course he'll ask me to mind the house for him, and keep the servants in order, and provide a different dinner every day, and all that; while you could go out to the neighbours' places to play lawn-tennis or cricket, and have lunch. It will be a very great responsibility.'

'What kind of dinners would you have?' said Mary.

Mrs Makebelieve's eye glistened, and she leaned forward in the bed; but just as she was about to reply the labouring man in the next room slammed his door, and went thundering down the stairs. In an instant Mrs Makebelieve bounded from her bed; three wide twists put up her hair; eight strange, billow-like movements put on her clothes; as each article of clothing reached a definite point on her person Mary stabbed it swiftly with a pin—four ordinary pins in this place, two safety-pins in that : then Mrs Makebelieve kissed her daughter sixteen times, and fled down the stairs and away to her work.

21

In a few minutes Mrs Cafferty came into the room. She was, as every woman is in the morning, primed with conversations about husbands; for in the morning husbands are unwieldy, morose creatures without joy, without lightness, lacking even the common, elemental interest in their own children, and capable of detestably misinterpreting the conversation of their wives. It is only by mixing amongst other men that this malignant humour may be dispelled. To them the company of men is like a great bath into which a husband will plunge wildly, renouncing as he dives wife and children, all anchors and securities of hearth and roof, and from which he again emerges singularly refreshed and capable of being interested by a wife, a family, and a home until the next morning. To many women this is a grievance amounting often to an affront, and although they endeavour, even by cooking, to heal the singular breach, they are utterly unable to do so, and perpetually seek the counsel of each other on the subject. Mrs Cafferty had merely asked her husband would he hold the baby while she poured out his stirabout, and he had incredibly threatened to pour the stirabout down the back of her neck if she didn't leave him alone.

It was upon this morning madness she had desired to consult her friend, and when she saw that Mrs Make-believe had gone away her disappointment was quite evident. But this was only for a moment. Almost all women are possessed of a fine social sense in relation to other women. They are always on their best behaviour towards one another. Indeed, it often seems as if they feared and must by all possible means placate each other by flattery, humour, or a serious tactfulness. There is very little freedom between them, because there is no real freedom or acquaintance but between things polar. There is nothing but a superficial resemblance between like and like, but between like and unlike there is space wherein both curiosity and spirit may go adventuring. Extremes must meet, it is their urgent necessity, the reason for their distance, and the greater the distance between them the swifter will be their return and the warmer their impact : they may shatter each other to fragments, or they may fuse and become indissoluble and new and wonderful, but there is no other fertility. Between the sexes there is a really extraordinary freedom of inter-course. They meet each other something more than half-way. A man and a woman may become quite intimate in a quarter of an hour. Almost certainly they will endeavour to explain themselves to each other before many minutes have elapsed; but a man and a man will not do this, and even less so will a woman and a woman, for these are the parallel lines which never meet. The acquaintanceship of the latter, in particular, often begins and ends in an armed and calculating neutrality. They preserve their distances and each other's sufferance by the exercise of a grave social tact which never deserts them, and which more than anything else has contributed to build the ceremonials which are nearly one-half of our civilisation. It is a common belief amongst men that women cannot live together without quarrelling, and that they are unable to get work done by other women with any of the good will which men display in the same occupations. If this is true, the reason should not be looked for in any intersexual complications, such as fear or an acrid rivalry, but only in the perpetually recurring physical disturbances to which, as a sex, they are subjected; and as the ability and willingness of a man to use his fists in response to an affront has imposed sobriety and good humour towards each other in almost all their relations, so women have placed barriers of politeness and ceremonial between their fellow-women and their own excoriated sensibilities.

Mrs Cafferty, therefore, dissembled her disappointment, and with an increased cordiality addressed herself towards Mary. Sitting down on the bedside, she discoursed on almost every subject upon which a woman may discourse. It is considered that the conversation of women, while incessant in its use, is rigorously bounded between the parlour and the kitchen, or, to be more precise, between the attic and the scullery; but these extremes are more inclusive than is imagined, for the attic has an outlook on the stars while the scullery usually opens on the kitchen garden or the dust-heap —vistas equal to horizons. The mysteries of death and birth occupy women far more than is the case with

76

men, to whom political and mercantile speculations are more congenial. With immediate buying and selling, and all the absolute forms of exchange and barter, women are deeply engaged, so that the realities of trade are often more intelligible to them than to many merchants. If men understood domestic economy half as well as women do, then their political economy and their entire consequent statecraft would not be the futile muddle which it is.

It was all very interesting to Mary, and, moreover, she had a great desire for companionship at the moment. If she had been left alone it might have become necessary to confront certain thoughts, memories, pictures, from which she had a dim idea it would be wise to keep her distance. Her work on the previous day, the girl she had met in the house, the policeman—from all or any of these recollections she swerved mentally. She steadily rejected all impressions that touched upon these. The policeman floated vaguely on her consciousness not as a desirable person, not even as a person, but as a distance, as an hour of her childhood, as a half-forgotten quaintness, a memory which it would be better should never be revived. Indeed, her faint thought shadowed him as a person who was dead, and would never again be visible to her anywhere. So, resolutely, she let him drop down into her mind to some uncomfortable oubliette from whence he threatened with feeble insistence to pop up at any moment like a strange question or a sudden shame. She hid him in a rosy flush which a breath could have made flame unbearably, and she hid from him behind the light garrulity of Mrs Cafferty, through which now and again, as through a veil, she saw the spike of his helmet, a wiry, bristling moustache, a surge of great shoulders. On these ghostly indications she heaped a tornado of words which swamped the wraith, but she knew he was waiting to catch her alone, and would certainly catch her, and the knowledge made her hate him.

77

22

Mrs Cafferty suggested that she and Mary should go out together to purchase that day's dinner, and by the time she had draped her shoulders in a shawl, buried her head in a bonnet, cautioned all her brood against going near the fireplace, the coal-box, and the slop-bucket, cut a slice of bread for each of them, and placed each of them in charge of all the rest, Mary's more elaborate dressing was within two stages of her hat.

'Wait until you have children, my dear,' said Mrs Cafferty, 'you won't be so pernickety then.' She further told Mary that when she was herself younger she had often spent an hour and a half doing up her hair, and she had been so particular that the putting on of a blouse or the pinning of a skirt to a belt had tormented her happily for two hours. 'But, bless you,' she roared, 'you get out of all that when you get children. Wait till you have six of them to be dressed every morning, and they with some of their boots lost and the rest of them mixed up, and each of them wriggling like an eel on a pan until you have to slap the devil out of them before their stocking can be got on: the way they screw their toes up in the wrong places! and the way they squeal that you're pinching them! and the way that they say you've rubbed soap on their eyes!'—Mrs Cafferty lifted her eyes and her hands to the ceiling in a dumb remonstrance with Providence, and dropped them again forlornly as one in whom Providence had never been really interested—'you'll have all the dressing you want, and a bit over for luck,' said she.

She complimented Mary on her hair, her complexion, the smallness of her feet, the largeness of her eyes, the slenderness of her waist, the width of her hat and of her shoestrings : so impartially and inclusively did she compliment her that by the time they went out Mary was rosy with appreciation and as self-confident as a young girl is entitled to be.

It was a beautiful grey day, with a massy sky which seemed as if it never could move again or change, and, as often happens in Ireland in cloudy weather. the air was so very clear that one could see to a great distance. On such days everything stands out in sharp outline. A street is no longer a congeries of houses huddling shamefully together and terrified lest any one should look at them and laugh. Each house then recaptures its individuality. The very roadways are aware of themselves, and bear their horses and cars and trams in a competent spirit, adorned with modesty as with a garland. It has a beauty beyond sunshine, for sunshine is only youth and carelessness. The impress of a thousand memories, the quiet face which experience has ripened into knowledge and mellowed into the wisdom of charity is seen then; the great social beauty shines from the streets under this sky that broods like a thoughtful forehead.

While they walked Mrs Cafferty planned, as a general might, her campaign of shopping. Her shopping differed greatly from Mrs Makebelieve's, and the difference was probably caused by her necessity to feed and clothe eight people as against Mrs Makebelieve's two. Mrs Makebelieve went to the shop nearest her house, and there entered into a staunch personal friendship with the proprietor. When she was given anything of doubtful value or material she instantly returned and handed it back, and the prices which were first quoted to her and settled upon became to Mrs Makebelieve an unalterable standard from which no departure would be tolerated. Eggs might go up in price for the remainder of the world, but not for her. A change of price threw Mrs Makebelieve into so wide-eyed, so galvanic, so powerfully-verbal and friendship-shattering an anger that her terms were accepted and registered as Median exactitudes. Mrs Cafferty, on the other hand, knew shopkeepers as personal enemies and as foes to the human race, who were bent on despoiling the poor, and against whom a remorseless warfare should be conducted by all decent people. Her knowledge of material, of quality, of degrees of freshness, of local and distant prices was profound. In Clanbrassil Street she would quote the prices of Moore Street with shattering effect, and if the shopkeeper declined to revise his tariff her good-humoured voice toned so huge a disapproval that other intending purchasers left the shop impressed by the unmasking of a swindler. Her method was abrupt. She seized an article, placed it on the counter, and uttered these words, 'Sixpence and not a penny more; I can get it in Moore Street for fivepence halfpenny'. She knew all the shops having a cheap line in some special article, and, therefore, her shopping was of a very extended description; not that she went from point to point, for she continually departed from the line of battle with the remark, 'Let's try what they have here', and when inside the shop her large eye took in at a glance a thousand details of stock and price which were never afterwards forgotten.

Mrs Cafferty's daughter, Norah, was going to celebrate her first Communion in a few days. This is a very important ceremony for a young girl and for her mother. A white muslin dress and a blue sash, a white muslin hat with blue ribbons, tan shoes, and stockings as germane to the colour of tan as may be—these all have to be provided. It is a time of grave concern for everybody intimately connected with the event. Every girl in the world has performed this ceremony : they have all been clad in these garments and shoes, and for a day or so all women, of whatever age, are in love with the little girl making her first Communion. Perhaps more than anything else it swings the passing stranger back to the time when she was not a woman but a child with present gaiety and curiosity, and a future all expectation and adventure. Therefore, the suitable apparelling of one's daughter is a public duty, and every mother endeavours to do the thing that is right, and live, if only for one day, up to the admiration of her fellow-creatures.

It was a trial, but an enjoyable one, to Mrs Cafferty and Mary this matching of tan stockings with tan shoes. The shoes were bought, and then an almost impossible quest began to find stockings which would exactly go with them. Thousands of boxes were opened, ransacked, and waved aside without the absolute colour being discovered. From shop to shop and from street to street they went, and the quest led through Grafton Street *en route* to a shop where, months before, Mrs Cafferty had seen stockings of a colour so nearly approximating to tan that they almost might be suitable.

As they went past the College and entered the winding street Mary's heart began to beat. She did not see any of the traffic flowing up and down, or the jostling, busy foot-passengers, nor did she hear the eager lectures of her companion. Her eyes were straining up the street towards the crossing. She dared not turn back or give any explanation to Mrs Cafferty, and in a few seconds she saw him, gigantic, calm, and adequate monarch of his world. His back was turned to her, and the great sweep of his shoulders, his solid legs, his red neck, and close-cropped, wiry hair were visible to her strangely. She had a peculiar feeling of acquaintness and of aloofness; intimate knowledge and a separation of sharp finality caused her to stare at him with so intent a curiosity that Mrs Cafferty noticed it.

'That's a fine man,' said she; 'he won't have to go about looking for girls.'

As she spoke they passed by the policeman, and Mary knew that when her eyes left him his gaze almost automatically fell upon her. She was glad that he could not see her face. She was glad that Mrs Cafferty was beside her : had she been alone she would have been tempted to walk away very quickly, almost to run, but her companion gave her courage and self-possession, so that she walked gallantly. But her mind was a fever. She could feel his eyes raking her from head to foot; she could see his great hand going up to tap his crinkly moustache. These things she could see in her terrified mind, but she could not think, she could only give thanks to God because she had her best clothes on.

23

Mrs Makebelieve was planning to get back such of her furniture and effects as had been pawned during her illness. Some of these things she had carried away from her father's house many years before when she got married. They had been amongst the earliest objects on which her eyes had rested when she was born, and around them her whole life of memories revolved : a chair in which her father had sat, and on the edge whereof her husband had timidly balanced himself when he came courting her, and into which her daughter had been tied when she was a baby. A strip of carpet and some knives and forks had formed portion of her wedding presents. She loved these things, and had determined that if work could retrieve them they should not be lost for ever. Therefore, she had to suffer people like Mrs O'Connor, not gladly, but with the resignation due to the hests of Providence which one must obey but may legitimately criticise. Mrs Makebelieve said definitely that she detested the woman. She was a cold-eyed person whose only ability was to order about other people who were much better than she was. It distressed Mrs Makebelieve to have to work for such a person, to be subject to her commands and liable to her reproofs or advice; these were things which seemed to her to be out of all due proportion. She did not wish the woman any harm, but some day or other she would undoubtedly have to put her in her proper place. It was a day to which she looked forward. Any one who had a sufficient income could have a house and could employ and pay for outside help without any particular reason for being proud, and many people, having such an income, would certainly have a better appointed house and would be more generous and civil to those who came to work for them. Everybody, of course, could not have a policeman for a nephew, and there were a great many people who would rather not have anything to do with a policeman at all. Overbearing, rough creatures to whom everybody is a thief! If Mrs Makebelieve had such a nephew she would certainly have wrecked his pride—the great beast! Here Mrs Makebelieve grew very angry : her black eyes blazed, her great nose grew thin and white, and her hands went leaping in fury. ' "You're not in Court now, you jackanapes you," said I—with his whiskers, and his baton, and his feet that were bigger than anything in the world except his ignorant self-conceit. "Have you a daughter, ma'am?" said he. "What's her age, ma'am?" said he. "Is she a good girl, ma'am?" said he.' But she had settled him. 'And that woman was prouder of him than a king would be of his crown! Never mind,' said Mrs Makebelieve, and she darted fiercely up and down the room, tearing pieces off the atmosphere and throwing them behind her.

In a few minutes, however, she sat down on the floor and drew her daughter's head to her breast, and then, staring into the scrap of fire, she counselled Mary wisely on many affairs of life and the conduct of a girl under all kinds of circumstances—to be adequate in spirit if not physique : that was her theme. Never to be a servant in your heart, said she. To work is nothing; the king on his throne, the priest kneeling before the Holy Altar, all people in all places had to work, but no person at all need be a servant. One worked and was paid, and went away keeping the integrity of one's soul unspotted and serene. If an employer was wise or good or kind, Mrs Makebelieve was prepared to accord such a person instant and humble reverence. She would work for such a one until the nails dropped off her fingers and her feet crumpled up under her body; but a policeman, or a rich person, or a person who ordered one about . . . ! until she died and was buried in the depths of the world, she would never give in to such a person or admit anything but their thievishness and ill-breeding. Bad manners to the like of them! said she, and might have sailed boisterously away upon an ocean of curses, but that Mary turned her face closer to her breast and began to speak.

For suddenly there had come to Mary a vision of peace : like a green island in the sea it was, like a white cloud on a broiling day; the sheltered life where all mundane preoccupations were far away, where ambition and hope and struggle were incredibly distant foolishness. Lowly and peaceful and unjaded was that life : she could see the nuns pacing quietly in their enclosed gardens, fingering their beads as they went to and fro and praying noiselessly for the sins of the world, or walking with solemn happiness to the Chapel to praise God in their own small companies, or going with hidden feet through the great City to nurse the sick and comfort those who had no other comforter than God—to pray in a quiet place, and not to be afraid any more or doubtful or despised . . . ! These things she saw and her heart leaped to them, and of these things she spoke to her mother, who listened with a tender smile and stroked her hair and hands. But her mother did not approve of these things. She spoke of nuns with reverence and affection. Many a gentle, sweet woman had she known of that sisterhood, many a one before whom she could have abased herself with tears and love, but such a life of shelter and restraint could never have been hers, nor did she believe it could be Mary's. For her a woman's business was life; the turmoil and strife of it was good to be in; it was a cleansing and a bracing. God did not need any assistance, but man did, bitterly he wanted it, and the giving of such assistance was the proper business of a woman. Everywhere there was a man to be helped, and the quest of a woman was to find the man who most needed her aid, and having found, to cleave to him for ever. In most of the trouble of life she divined men and women not knowing or not doing their duty, which was to love one another and to be neighbourly and obliging to their fellows. A partner, a home and children—through the loyal co-operation of these she saw happiness and, dimly, a design of so vast an architecture as scarcely to be discussed. The bad and good of humanity moved her to an equal ecstasy of displeasure and approbation, but her God was Freedom and her religion Love. Freedom! even the last rags of it that remain to a regimented world! That was a passion with her. She must order her personal life without any ghostly or bodily supervision. She would oppose an encroachment on that with her nails and her teeth, and this last fringe of freedom was what nuns had sacrificed and all servants and other people had bartered away. One must work, but one must never be a slave—these laws seemed to her equally imperative; the structure of the world swung upon them, and whoever violated these laws was a traitor to both God and man.

But Mary did not say anything. Her mother's arms were around her, and suddenly she commenced to cry upon a bosom that was not strange. There was surely healing in that breast of love, a rampart of tenderness against the world, a door which would never be closed against her or opened to her enemies.

24

In a little city like Dublin one meets every person whom one knows within a few days. Around each bend in the road there is a friend, an enemy, or a bore striding towards you, so that, with a piety which is almost religious, one says 'touch wood' before turning any corner. It was not long, therefore, until Mary again met the big policeman. He came up behind her and walked by her side, chatting with a pleasant ease, in which, however, her curious mind could discover some obscure distinctions. On looking backwards it seemed to Mary that he had always come from behind her, and the retrospect dulled his glory to the diminishing point. For indeed his approach was too consistently policeman-like, it was too crafty; his advent hinted at a gross espionage, at a mind which was no longer a man's but a detective's, who tracked everybody by instinct, and arrested his friends instead of saluting them.

As they walked along Mary was in a fever of discomfort. She wished dumbly that the man would go away, but for the wealth of the world she could not have brought herself to hurt the feelings of so big a man. To endanger the very natural dignity of a big man was a thing which no woman could do without a pang; the shame of it made her feel hot : he might have blushed or stammered, and the memory of that would sting her miserably for weeks as though she had insulted an elephant or a baby.

She could not get away from him. She had neither the courage nor the experience which enables a woman to dismiss a man without wounding him, and so, perforce, she continued walking by his side while he treated her to an intelligent dissertation on current political events and the topography of the City of Dublin.

But, undoubtedly, there was a change in the policeman, and it was not difficult to account for. He was more easy and familiar in his speech : while formerly he had bowed as from the peaks of manly intellect to the pleasant valleys of girlish incompetence, he now condescended from the loftiness of a policeman and a person of quality to the quaint gutters of social inferiority. To many people mental inferiority in a companion has a charm, for it induces in one's proper person a feeling of philosophic detachment, a fine effect of personal individuality and superiority which is both bracing and uplifting—there is not any particular harm in this : progress can be, and is, accelerated by the hypocrisies and snobbishness, all the minor, unpleasant adjuncts of mediocrity. Snobbishness is a puling infant, but it may grow to a deeply whiskered ambition, and most virtues are, on examination, the amalgam of many vices. But while intellectual poverty may be forgiven and loved, social inequality can only be utilised. Our fellows, however addled, are our friends, our inferiors are our prey, and since the policeman had discovered Mary publicly washing out an alien hall his respect for her had withered and dropped to death almost in an instant; whence it appears that there is really only one grave and debasing vice in the world, and that is poverty.

In many ways the distinction and the difference were apparent to Mary. The dignity of a gentleman and a man of the world was partly shorn away : the gentleman portion, which comprised kindness and reticence, had vanished; the man of the world remained, typified by a familiarity which assumed that this and that, understood but not to be mentioned, shall be taken for granted; a spurious equalisation perched jauntily but insecurely on a non-committal, and that base flattery which is the only coin wherewith a thief can balance his depredations. For as they went pacing down a lonely road towards the Dodder the policeman diversified his entertaining lore by a succession of compliments which ravaged the heavens and the earth and the deep sea for a fitting symbology. Mary's eyes and the gay heavens were placed in juxtaposition and the heavens were censured, the vegetable, animal, and mineral worlds were discomfited, the deep sea sustained a reproof, and the by-products of nature and of art drooped into a nothingness too vast even for laughter. Mary had not the slightest objection to hearing that all other women in the world seemed cripples and gargoyles when viewed against her

87

own transcendent splendour, and she was prepared to love the person who said this innocently and happily. She would have agreed to be an angel or a queen to a man demanding potentates and powers in his sweetheart, and would joyfully have equalised matters by discovering the buried god in her lover and believing in it as sincerely as he permitted—but this man was not saying the truth. She could see him making the things up as he talked. There was eagerness in him, but no spontaneity. It was not even eagerness, it was greediness : he wanted to eat her up and go away with her bones sticking out of his mouth as the horns of a deer protrude from the jaws of an anaconda, veritable evidence to it and his fellows of a victory and an orgy to command respect and envy. But he was familiar, he was complacent, and—amazedly she discovered it—he was big. Her vocabulary could not furnish her with the qualifying word, or rather epithet, for his bigness. Horrible was suggested and retained, but her instinct clamoured that there was a fat, oozy word somewhere which would have brought comfort to her brains and her hands and feet. He did not keep his arms quiet, but tapped his remarks into her blouse and her shoulder. Each time his hands touched her they remained a trifle longer. They seemed to be great red spiders, they would grip her all round and squeeze her clammily while his face spiked her to death with its moustache. . . . And he smiled also, he giggled and cut capers; his language now was a perpetual witticism at which he laughed in jerks, and at which she laughed tightly like an obedient, quick echo : and then, suddenly, without a word, in a dazing flash, his arms were about her. There was nobody in sight at all, and he was holding her like a great spider, and his bristly moustache darted forward to spike her to death, and then, somehow, she was free, away from him, scudding down the road lightly and fearfully and very swiftly. 'Wait, wait,' he called—'wait!' But she did not wait.

25

Mrs Cafferty came in that evening for a chat with Mrs Makebelieve. There were traces of worry on the lady's face, and she hushed the children who trooped in her wake with less of good humour than they were accustomed to. Instead of threatening to smack them on the head, as was usual, she did smack them, and she walked surrounded by lamentations as by a sea.

Things were not going at all well with her. There was a slackness in her husband's trade, so that for days together he was idle, and although the big woman amended her expenditure in every direction she could not by any means adjust eight robust appetites to a shrunken income. She explained her position to Mrs Makebelieve : children would not, they could not, consent to go on shorter rations than they had been accustomed to, and it seemed to her that daily, almost hourly, their appetites grew larger and more terrible. She showed her right hand whereon the mere usage of a bread-knife had scored a ridge which was now a permanent disfigurement.

'God bless me,' she shouted angrily, 'what right have I to ask the creatures to go hungry? Am I to beat them when they cry? It's not their fault that they want food, and it's not my poor man's fault that they haven't any. He's ready to work at his trade if anybody wants him to do so, and if he can't get work, and if the children are hungry, whose fault is it?'

Mrs Cafferty held that there was something wrong somewhere, but whether the blame was to be allocated to the weather, the employer, the Government, or the Deity, she did not know, nor did Mrs Makebelieve know; but they were agreed that there was an error somewhere, a lack of adjustment with which they had nothing to do, but the effects whereof were grievously visible in their privations. Meantime it had become necessary that Mrs Cafferty should adjust herself to a changing environment. A rise or fall in wages is automatically followed by a similar enlargement or shrinkage of one's necessities, and the consequent difference is registered at all points of one's life-contact. The physical and mental activities of a well-to-do person can reach out to a horizon, while those of very poor people are limited to their immediate, stagnant atmosphere, and so the lives of a vast portion of society are liable to a ceaseless change, a flux swinging from good to bad for ever, an expansion and constriction against which they have no safeguards and not even any warning. In free nature this problem is paralleled by the shrinking and expansion of the seasons; the summer ith its wealth of food, the winter following after with its famine; but many wild creatures are able to make a thrifty provision against the bad time which they know comes as certainly and periodically as the good times. Bees and squirrels and many others fill their barns with the plentiful overplus of the summer fields; birds can migrate and find sunshine and sustenance elsewhere; and others again can store during their good season a life energy by means whereof they may sleep healthily through their hard times. These organisations can be adjusted to their environment because the changes of the latter are known and can be more or less accurately predicted from any point. But the human worker has no such regularity. His food period does not ebb and recur with the seasons. There is no periodicity in their changes, and, therefore, no possibility for defensive or protective action. His physical structure uses and excretes energy so rapidly that he cannot store it up and go to sleep on his savings, and his harvests are usually so lean and disconnected that the exercise of thrift is equally an impossibility and a mockery. The life, therefore, of such a person is composed of a constant series of adjustments and readjustments, and the stern ability wherewith these changes are met and combated are more admirably ingenious than the much-praised virtues of ants and bees to which they are constantly directed as to exemplars.

Mrs Cafferty had now less money than she had been used to, but she had still the same rent to pay, the same number of children to feed, and the same personal dignity to support as in her better days, and her problem was to make up, by some means to which she was a stranger, the money which had drifted beyond the reach of her husband. The methods by which she could do this were very much restricted. Children require an attention which occupies the entire of a mother's time, and, consequently, she was prevented from seeking abroad any mitigation of her hardships. The occupations which might be engaged in at home were closed to her by mere overwhelming competition. The number of women who are prepared to make ten million shirts for a penny is already far in excess of the demand, and so, except by a severe undercutting such as a contract to make twenty million shirts for a halfpenny, work of this description is very difficult to obtain.

Under these circumstances nothing remained for Mrs Cafferty but to take in a lodger. This is a form of co-operation much practised among the poorer people. The margin of direct profit accruing from such a venture is very small, but this is compensated for by the extra spending power achieved. A number of people pooling their money in this way can buy to greater advantage and in a cheaper market than is possible to the solitary purchaser, and a moderate toll for wear and tear and usage, or, as it is usually put, for rent and attendance, gives the small personal profit at which such services are reckoned.

Through the good offices of a neighbouring shopkeeper Mrs Cafferty had secured a lodger, and, with the courage which is never separate from despair, she had rented a small room beside her own. This room, by an amazing economy of construction, contained a fireplace and a window : it was about one square inch in diameter, and was undoubtedly a fine room. The lodger was to enter into possession on the following day, and Mrs Cafferty said he was a very nice young man indeed and did not drink.

26

Mrs Cafferty's lodger duly arrived. He was young and as thin as a lath, and he moved with fury. He was seldom in the place at all : he fled into the house for his food, and having eaten it, he fled away from the house again, and did not reappear until it was time to go to bed. What he did with himself in the interval Mrs Cafferty did not know, but she was prepared to wager her soul, the value of which she believed was high, on the fact that he was a good young man who never gave the slightest trouble, saving that his bedclothes were always lying on the floor in the morning, and there was candle grease on one corner of his pillow, and that he cleaned his boots on a chair. But these were things which one expected a young man to do, and the omission of them might have caused one to look curiously at the creature and to doubt his masculinity.

Mrs Makebelieve replied that habits of order and neatness were rarely to be found in young people of either sex; more especially were these absent in boys who are released in early youth by their mothers from all purely domestic employments. A great many people believed, and she believed herself, that it was not desirable a man or boy should conform too rigidly to household rules. She had observed that the comfort of a home was lost to many men if they were expected to take their boots off when they came into the house, or to hang their hats up in a special place. The women of a household, being so constantly indoors, find it easy and businesslike to obey the small rules which comprise household legislation, but as the entire policy of a house was to make it habitable and comfortable for its men folk, all domestic ordinances might be strained to the uttermost until the compromise was found to mollify even exceptional idiosyncrasies. A man, she held, bowed to quite sufficient discipline during his working hours, and his home should be a place free from every vexatious restraint and wherein he might enjoy as wide a liberty as was good for him.

These ideas were applauded by Mrs Cafferty, and she supplemented them by a recital of how she managed her own husband, and of the ridiculous ease whereby any man may be governed; for she had observed that men were very susceptible to control if only the control was not too apparent. If a man did a thing twice, the doing of that thing became a habit and a passion, any interference with which provoked him to an unreasoning, bull-like wrath wherein both wives and crockery were equally shattered; and, therefore, a woman had only to observe the personal habits of her beloved and fashion her restrictions according to that standard. This meant that men made the laws and women administered them—a wise allocation of prerogatives, for she conceived that the executive female function was every whit as important as the creative faculty which brought these laws into being. She was quite prepared to leave the creative powers in male hands if they would equally abstain from interference with the subsequent working details, for she was of opinion that in the pursuit of comfort (not entirely to their credit was it said) men were far more anxiously concerned than were women, and they flew to their bourne with an instinct for short cuts wherewith women were totally unacquainted.

But in the young man who had come to lodge with her Mrs Cafferty discerned a being in whom virtue had concentrated to a degree that almost amounted to a congestion. He had instantly played with the children on their being presented to him : this was the sign of a good nature. Before he was acquainted with her ten minutes he had made four jokes : this was the sign of a pleasant nature; and he sang loudly and unceasingly when he awoke in the morning, which was the unfailing index to a happy nature. Moreover, he ate the meals provided for him without any of that particular, tedious examination which is so insulting, and had complimented Mrs Cafferty on an ability to put a taste on food which she was pleased to obtain recognition of.

Both Mary and her mother remarked on these details with an admiration which was as much as either politeness or friendship could expect. Mrs Makebelieve's solitary method of life had removed her so distantly from youth that information about a young man was almost tonic to her. She had never wished for a second husband, but had often fancied that a son would have been a wonderful joy to her. She considered that a house which had no young man growing up in it was not a house at all, and she believed that a boy would love his mother, if not more than a daughter could, at least with a difference which would be strangely sweet—a rash, impulsive, unquiet love; a love which would continually prove her love to the breaking point; a love that demanded, and demanded with careless assurance, that accepted her goodness as unquestioningly as she accepted the fertility of the earth, and used her knowing blindly and flatteringly how inexhaustively rich her depths were. . . . She could have wept for this; it was priceless beyond kingdoms; the smile on a boy's face lifted her to an exaltation. Her girl was inexpressibly sweet, surely an island in her wide heart, but a little boy . . . her breasts could have filled with milk for him, him she could have nourished in the rocks and in desert places : he would have been life to her and adventure, a barrier against old age, an incantation against sorrow, a fragrance and a grief and a defiance.

It was quite plain that Mrs Cafferty was satisfied with this addition to her household, but the profit which she had expected to accrue from his presence was not the liberal one she had in mind when making the preliminary arrangements. For it appeared that the young man had an appetite of which Mrs Cafferty spoke with the respect proper to something colossal and awesome. A half-loaf did not more than break the back of a hunger which could wriggle disastrously over another half-loaf; so that, instead of being relieved by his advent, she was confronted by a more immediate and desolating bankruptcy than that from which she had attempted to escape. Exactly how to deal with this situation she did not know, and it was really in order to discuss her peculiar case that she had visited Mrs Makebelieve. She could, of course, have approached the young man and demanded from him an increase of money that would still be equitable to both parties, but she confessed a repugnance to this course. She did not like to upbraid or trouble any one on account of an appetite which was so noteworthy. She disliked, in any event, to raise a question about food : her instinct for hospitality was outraged at the thought, and as she was herself the victim, or the owner, of an appetite which had often placed a strain on her revenues, a fellow-feeling operated still further in mitigation of his disqualification.

Mrs Makebelieve's advice was that she should stifle the first fierce and indiscriminate cravings of the young man's hunger by a liberal allowance of stirabout, which was a cheap, wholesome, and very satisfying food, and in that way his destruction of more costly victuals would be kept within reasonable limits. Appetite, she held, was largely a matter of youth, and as a boy who was scarcely done growing had no way of modifying his passion for nourishment, it would be a lapse from decency to insult him on so legitimate a failing.

Mrs Cafferty thought that this might be done, and thanked her friend for the counsel; but Mary, listening

to these political matters, conceived Mrs Cafferty as a
person who had no longer any claim to honour, and she
pitied the young man whose appetite was thus publicly
canvassed, and who might at any moment be turned out
of house and home on account of a hunger against
which he had no safeguard and no remedy.

27

It was not long until Mary and Mrs Cafferty's lodger
met. As he came in by the hall-door one day Mary was
carrying upstairs a large water-bucket, the portage of
which two or three times a day is so heavy a strain on
the dweller in tenements. The youth instantly seized the
bucket, and despite her protestations and appeals, he
carried it upstairs. He walked a few steps in advance
of Mary, whistling cheerfully as he went, so she was
able to get a good view of him. He was so thin that he
nearly made her laugh, but he carried the bucket the
weight of which she had often bowed under, with an
ease astonishing in so slight a man, and there was a
spring in his walk which was pleasant to see. He laid the
bucket down outside her room, and requested her
urgently to knock at his door whenever she required
more water fetched, because he would be only too
delighted to do it for her, and it was not the slightest
trouble in the world. While he spoke he was stealing
glances at her face and Mary was stealing glances at
his face, and when they caught one another doing this
at the same moment they both looked hurriedly away,
and the young man departed to his own place.

But Mary was very angry with this young man. She
had gone downstairs in her house attire, which was not
resplendent, and she objected to being discovered by
any youth in raiment not suitable to such an occasion.

She could not visualise herself speaking to a man unless she was adorned as for a festivity. The gentlemen and ladies of whom her mother sometimes spoke, and of whom she had often dreamt, were never mean in their habiliments. The gentlemen frequently had green silken jackets with a foam of lace at the wrists and a cascade of the same rich material brawling upon their breasts, and the ladies were attired in a magnificent scarcity of clothing, the fundamental principle whereof, although she was quite assured of its righteousness, she did not yet understand.

Indeed, at this period Mary's interest in dress far transcended any interest she had ever known before. She knew intimately the window contents of every costumier's shop in Grafton and Wicklow and Dawson Streets, and could follow with intelligent amazement the apparently trifling, but exceedingly important, differences of line or seam or flounce which ranked one garment as a creation and its neighbour as a dress. She and her mother often discussed the gowns wherein the native dignity of their souls might be adequately caparisoned. Mrs Makebelieve, with a humility which had still a trace of anger, admitted that the period when she could have been expressed in colour had expired, and she decided that a black silk dress, with a heavy gold chain falling along the bosom, was as much as her soul was now entitled to. She had an impatience, amounting to contempt, for those florid, flamboyant souls whose outer physical integument so grievously misrepresented them. She thought that after a certain time one should dress the body and not the soul, and, discovering an inseparability between the two, she held that the mean shrine must hold a very trifling deity and that an ill-made or time-worn body should never dress gloriously under pain of an accusation of hypocrisy or foolishness.

But for Mary she planned garments with a freedom and bravery which astonished while it delighted her daughter. She combined twenty styles into one style of terrifying originality. She conceived dresses of a complexity beyond the labour of any but a divinely inspired needle, and others again whose simplicity was almost too tenuous for human speech. She discussed robes whose trailing and voluminous richness could with difficulty be supported by ten strong attendants, and she had heard of a dress and fabric whereof was of such gossamer and ethereal insubstancy that it might be packed into a walnut more conveniently than an ordinary dress could be impressed into a portmanteau. Mary's exclamations of delight and longing ranged from every possible dress to every impossible one, and then Mrs Makebelieve reviewed all the dresses she had worn from the age of three years to the present day, including wedding and mourning dresses, those which were worn at picnics and dances and for travelling, with an occasional divergence which comprehended the clothing of her friends and her enemies during the like period. She explained the basic principles of dress to her daughter, showing that in this art, as in all else, order cannot be dispensed with. There were things a tall person might wear, but which a short person might not, and the draperies which adorned a portly lady were but pitiable weeds when trailed by her attenuated sister. The effect of long, thin lines in a fabric will make a short woman appear tall, while round, thick lines can reduce the altitude of people whose height is a trouble to be combated. She illustrated the usage of large and small checks and plaids and all the mazy interweaving of other cloths, and she elucidated the mystery of colour, tone, halftone, light and shade so interestingly that Mary could scarcely hear enough of her lore. She was acquainted with the colours which a dark person may wear and those which are suitable to a fair person, and the shades proper to be used by the wide class ranging between these extremes she knew also, with a special provision for red-haired and sandy folk and those who have no complexion at all. Certain laws which she formulated

were cherished by her daughter as oracular utterances—
that one should match one's eyes in the house and one's
hair in the street, was one; that one's hat and gloves and
shoes were of vastly more importance than all the rest
of one's clothing, was another; that one's hair and
stockings should tone as nearly as possible, was a third.
Following these rules, she assured her daughter, a
woman could never be other than well dressed, and all
of these things Mary learned by heart and asked her
mother to tell her more, which her mother was quite
able and willing to do.

28

When the sexual instinct is aroused, men and dogs and
frogs and beetles, and such other creatures as are inside
or outside of this catalogue, are very tenacious in the
pursuit of their ambition. We can seldom get away from
that which attracts or repels us. Love and hate are
equally magnetic and compelling, and each, being super-
normal, drags us willingly or woefully in its wake, until
at last our blind persistency is either routed or appeased,
and we advance our lauds or gnash our teeth as the
occasion bids us. There is no tragedy more woeful than
the victory of hate, nor any attainment so hopelessly
barren as the sterility of that achievement; for hate is
finality, and finality is the greatest evil which can happen in a world of movement. Love is an inaugurator
displaying his banners on captured peaks and pressing
for ever to a new and more gracious enterprise, but the
victories of hate are gained in a ditch from which there
is no horizon visible, and whence there does not go even
one limping courier.

After Mary fled from the embrace of the great policeman he came to think more closely of her than he had

been used; but her image was throned now in anger: she came to him like a dull brightness wherefrom desolate thunder might roll at an instant. Indeed, she began to obsess him so that not even the ministrations of his aunt nor the obeisances of that pleasant girl, the name of whose boots was Fairybell, could give him any comfort or wean him from a contemplation which sprawled gloomily between him and his duties to the traffic. If he had not discovered the lowliness of her quality his course might have been simple and straightforward: the issue, in such event, would have narrowed to every man's poser—whether he should marry this girl or that girl?—but the arithmetic whereby such matters are elucidated would at the last have eased his perplexity, and the path indicated could have been followed with the fullest freedom on his part and without any disaster to his self-love. If, whichever way his inclination wavered, there was any pang of regret (and there was bound to be), such a feeling would be ultimately waived by his reason or retained as a memorial which had a gratifying savour. But the knowledge of Mary's social inferiority complicated matters, for, although this automatically put her out of the question as his wife, her subsequent ill-treatment of himself had injected a virus to his blood which was one-half a passion for her body and one-half a frenzy for vengeance. He could have let her go easily enough if she had not first let him go; for he read dismissal in her action and resented it as a trespass on his own just prerogative. He had but to stretch out his hand and she would have dropped to it as tamely as a kitten, whereas now she eluded his hand, would, indeed, have nothing to do with it; and this could not be forgiven. He would gladly have beaten her into submission, for what right has a slip of a girl to withstand the advances of a man and a policeman? That is a crooked spirit demanding to be straightened with a truncheon: but as we cannot decently, or even peaceably, beat a girl until she is married to us, he had to relinquish that dear idea.

He would have dismissed her from his mind with the contempt she deserved, but, alas! he could not : she clung there like a burr, not to be dislodged saving by possession or a beating—two shuddering alternatives— for she had become detestably dear to him. His senses and his self-esteem conspired to heave her to a pedestal where his eye strained upwards in bewilderment—that she who was below him could be above him! This was astounding : she must be pulled from her eminence and stamped back to her native depths by his own indignant hoofs; thence she might be gloriously lifted again with a calm, benignant, masculine hand shedding pardons and favours, and perhaps a mollifying unguent for her bruises. Bruises! a knee, an elbow—they were nothing; little damages which to kiss was to make well again. Will not women cherish a bruise that it may be medicined by male kisses? Nature and precedent have both sworn to it. . . . But she was out of reach; his hand, high-flung as it might be, could not get to her. He went furiously to the Phoenix Park, to St Stephen's Green, to outlying leafy spots and sheltered lanes, but she was in none of these places. He even prowled about the neighbourhood of her home and could not meet her. Once he had seen Mary as she came along the road, and he drew back into a doorway. A young man was marching by her side, a young man who gabbled without ceasing and to whom Mary chattered again with an equal volubility. As they passed by Mary caught sight of him, and her face went flaming. She caught her companion's arm, and they hurried down the road at a great pace. . . . She had never chattered to him. Always he had done the talking, and she had been an obedient, grateful listener. Nor did he quarrel with her silence, but her reserve shocked him; it was a pretence—worse, a lie—a masked and hooded falsehood. She had surrendered to him willingly, and yet drew about her a protective armour of reserve wherein she skulked immune to the arms which were lawfully victorious. Is there, then, no loot for a

101

conqueror? We demand the keys of the City Walls and unrestricted entry, or our torches shall blaze again. This chattering Mary was a girl whom he had never caught sight of at all. She had been hiding from him even in his presence. In every aspect she was an anger. But she could talk to the fellow with her . . . a skinny whipper-snapper, whom the breath of a man could shred into remote, eyeless vacuity. Was this man another insult? Did she not even wait to bury her dead? Pah! she was not value for his thought. A girl so lightly facile might be blown from here to there and she would scarcely notice the difference. Here and there were the same places to her, and him and him were the same person. A girl of that type comes to a bad end : he had seen it often, the type and the end, and never separate. Can one not prophesy from facts? He saw a slut in a slum, a drab hovering by a dark entry, and the vision cheered him mightily for one glowing minute and left him unoccupied for the next, into which she thronged with the flutter of wings and the sound of a great mocking.

His aunt tracked his brows back to the responsible duties of his employment, and commiserated with him, and made a lamentation about matters with which he never had been occupied, so that the last tag of his good manners departed from him, and he damned her unswervingly into consternation. That other pleasant girl, whose sweetness he had not so much tasted as sampled, had taken to brooding in his presence : she sometimes drooped an eye upon him like a question. . . . Let her look out or maybe he'd blaze into her teeth : howl menace down her throat until she swooned. Some one should yield to him a visible and tangible agony to balance his. Does law probe no deeper than the pillage of a watch? Can one filch our self-respect and escape free? Shall not our souls also sue for damages against its aggressor? Some person rich enough must pay for his lacerations or there was less justice in heaven than in the Police Courts; and it might be that girl's lot to

102

expiate the sins of Mary. It would be a pleasure, if a sour one, to make somebody wriggle as he had, and somebody should wriggle; of that he was blackly determined.

29

Indeed, Mrs Cafferty's lodger and Mary had become quite intimate, and it was not through the machinations of either that this had happened. Ever since Mrs Make-believe had heard of that young man's appetite, and the miseries through which he had to follow it, she had been deeply concerned on his behalf. She declined to believe that the boy ever got sufficient to eat, and she enlarged to her daughter on the seriousness of this privation to a young man. Disabilities, such as a young girl could not comprehend, followed in the train of insufficient nourishment. Mrs Cafferty was her friend, and was, moreover, a good decent woman against whom the tongue of rumour might wag in vain; but Mrs Cafferty was the mother of six children, and her natural kindliness dared not expand to their detriment. Furthermore, the fact of her husband being out of work tended to still further circumscribe the limits of her generosity. She divined a lean pot in the Cafferty household, and she saw the young man getting only as much food as Mrs Cafferty dared to give him, so that the pangs of his hunger gnawed at her own vitals. Under these circumstances she had sought for an opportunity to become better acquainted with him, and had very easily succeeded; so when Mary found him seated on their bed and eating violently of their half-loaf, if she was astonished at first she was also very glad. Her mother watched the demolition of their food with a calm happiness, for although the amount she could contribute was small, every little helped, and not alone were his wants assisted, but her friend Mrs Cafferty and her children were also aided by this dulling of an appetite which might have endangered their household peace.

The young man repaid their hospitality by an easy generosity of speech covering affairs which neither Mrs Makebelieve nor her daughter had many opportunities for studying. He spoke of those very interesting matters with which a young man is concerned, and his speculations on various subjects, while often quite ignorant, were sufficiently vivid to be interesting and were wrong in a boyish fashion which was not unpleasant. He was very argumentative, but was still open to reason; therefore Mrs Makebelieve had opportunities for discussion which were seldom granted to her. Insensibly she adopted the position of guide, philosopher, and friend to him; and Mary also found new interests in speech, for although the young man thought very differently from her, he did think upon her own plane, and the things which secretly engrossed him were also the things wherewith she was deeply preoccupied. A community of ignorances may be as binding as a community of interests. We have a dull suspicion of that him or her who knows more than we do, but the person who is prepared to go out adventuring with us, with surmise only for a chart and enjoyment for a guide, may use our hand as his own and our pockets as his treasury.

As the young man had no more shyness than a cat, it soon fell out that he and Mary took their evening walks together. He was a clerk in a large establishment, and had many things to tell Mary which were of great interest to both of them. For in his place of business he had both friends and enemies of whom he was able to speak with the fluency which was their due. Mary knew, for instance, that the chief was bald but decent (she could not believe that the connection was natural), and that the second in command had neither virtues nor whiskers. (She saw him as a codfish with a malignant eye.) He epitomised the vices which belonged in detail to the world, but were peculiar to himself in bulk. (He must be hairy in that event.) Language, even the young man's, could not describe him adequately. (He ate boys for breakfast and girls for tea.) With this person the young man was in eternal conflict (a bear with little ears and big teeth); not open conflict, for that would have meant instant dismissal (not hairy at all—a long, slimy eel with a lot of sense), but a veiled, unremitting warfare which occupied all their spare attention. The young man knew for an actual fact that some day he would be compelled to hit that chap, and it would be a sorry day for the fellow, because his ability to hit was startling. He told Mary of the evil results which had followed some of his blows, and Mary's incredulity was only heightened by a display of the young man's muscles. She extolled these because she thought it was her duty to do so, but preserved some doubts of their unique destructiveness. Once she asked him could he fight a policeman, and he assured her that policemen are not able to fight at all singly, but only in squads, when their warfare is callous and ugly and conducted mainly with their boots; so that decent people have no respect for their fighting qualities or their private characters. He assured her that not only could he fight a policeman, but he could also tyrannise over the seed, breed, and generation of such a one, and, moreover, he could accomplish this without real exertion. Against all policemen and soldiers the young man professed an eager hostility, and with these bad people he included landlords and many employers of labour. His denunciation of these folk might be traced back to the belief that none of them treated one fairly. A policeman, he averred, would arrest a man for next door to nothing, and any resistance offered to their spleen rendered the unfortunate prisoner liable to be manhandled in his cell until their outraged dignity was appeased. The three capital crimes upon which a man is liable to arrest are for being drunk, or disorderly, or for refusing to fight, and to these perils a young man is peculiarly susceptible, and is, to that extent, interested in the Force, and critical of their behaviour. The sight of a soldier annoyed him, for he saw a conqueror, trampling vaingloriously through the capital of his country, and the inability of his land to eject the braggart astonished and mortified him. Landlords had no bowels of compassion. There was no kindliness of heart among them, nor any wish to assist those whose whole existence was engaged on their behalf. He saw them as lazy, unproductive gluttons who cried for ever 'Give, give', and who gave nothing in return but an increased insolent tyranny. Many employers came into the same black category. They were people who had disowned all duty to humanity, and who saw in themselves the beginning and the end of all things. They gratified their acquisitiveness not in order that they might become benefactors of their kind (the only righteous freedom of which we know), but merely to indulge a petty exercise of power and to attain that approval which is granted to wealth and the giving of which is the great foolishness of mankind. These people used their helpers and threw them away; they exploited and bought and sold their fellowmen, while their arrogant self-assurance and the monstrous power which they had gathered for their security shocked him like a thing unbelievable in spite of its reality. That such things could be, fretted him into clamour. He wanted to point them out to all people. He saw his neighbours' ears clogged, and he was prepared to die howling if only he could pierce those encrusted auditories. That what was so simple to him should not be understood by everybody! He could see plainly and others could not, although their eyes looked straightly forward and veritably rolled with intent and consciousness! Did their eyes and ears and brains act differently to his, or was he a singular monster cursed from his birth with madness? At times he was prepared to let humanity and Ireland go to the devil their own way, he being well assured that without him they were bound quickly for deep perdition. Of Ireland he sometimes spoke with a fervour of passion which would be outrageous if addressed to a woman. Surely he saw her as a woman, queenly and distressed and very proud. He was physically anguished for her, and the man who loved her was the very brother of his bones. There were some words the effect of which were almost hypnotic on him —The Isle of the Blest, The Little Dark Rose, The Poor Old Woman, and Caitlin the Daughter of Houlihan. The mere repetition of these phrases lifted him to an ecstasy; they had hidden, magical meanings which pricked deeply to his heartstrings and thrilled him to a tempest of pity and love. He yearned to do deeds of valour, violent, grandiose feats which would redound to her credit and make the name of Irishmen synonymous with either greatness or singularity: for, as yet, the distinction between these words was no more clear to him than it is to any other young man who reads violence as heroism and eccentricity as genius. Of England he spoke with something like stupefaction: as a child cowering in a dark wood tells of the ogre who has slain his father and carried his mother away to a drear captivity in his castle of bones—so he spoke of England. He saw an Englishman stalking hideously forward with a princess tucked under each arm, while their brothers and their knights were netted in enchantment and slept heedless of the wrongs done to their ladies and of the defacement of their shields. . . . 'Alas, alas and alas, for the once proud people of Banba!'

30

Mrs Makebelieve was astonished when the policeman knocked at her door. A knock at her door was a rare sound, for many years had gone by since any one had

come to visit her. Of late Mrs Cafferty often came to
talk to her, but she never knocked; she usually shouted,
'Can I come in?' and then she came in. But this was a
ceremonious knock which startled her, and the spectacle
of the great man bending through the doorway almost
stopped her breath. Mary also was so shocked into terror that she stood still, forgetful of all good manners,
and stared at the visitor open-eyed. She knew and did
not know what he had come for; but that, in some
way, his appearance related to her she was instantly
assured, although she could not even dimly guess at a
closer explanation of his visit. His eyes stayed on her for
an instant and then passed to her mother, and, following her rather tremulous invitation, he came into the
room. There was no chair to sit on, so Mrs Makebelieve
requested him to sit down on the bed, which he did. She
fancied he had come on some errand from Mrs O'Connor, and was inclined to be angry at a visit which she
construed as an intrusion, so when he was seated, she
waited to hear what he might have to say.

Even to her it was evident that the big man was perplexed and abashed; his hat was in his way, and so were
his hands, and when he spoke his voice was so husky as
to be distressful. On Mary, who had withdrawn to the
very end of the room, this discomfort of speech had a
peculiar effect : the unsteady voice touched her breast
to a kindred fluttering, and her throat grew parched and
so irritated that a violent fit of coughing could not be
restrained, and this, with the nervousness and alarm
which his appearance had thronged upon her, drove her
to a very fever of distress. But she could not take her
eyes away from him, and she wondered and was afraid
of what he might say. She knew there were a great many
things he might discuss which she would be loath to hear
in her mother's presence, and which her mother would
not be gratified to hear either.

He spoke for a few moments about the weather, and
Mrs Makebelieve hearkened to his remarks with a per-

plexity which she made no effort to conceal. She was quite certain he had not called to speak about the weather, and she was prepared to tell him so if a suitable opportunity should occur. She was also satisfied that he had not come on a formal, friendly visit—the memory of her last interview with him forbade such a conjecture, for on that occasion politeness had been deposed from her throne and acrimony had reigned in her stead. If his aunt had desired him to undertake an embassy to her he would surely have delivered his message without preamble, and would not have been thrown by so trifing a duty into the state of agitation in which he was. It was obvious, therefore, that he had not come with a message relating to her work. Something of fear touched Mrs Makebelieve as she looked at him, and her voice had an uneasy note when she requested to know what she could do for him.

The policeman suddenly, with the gesture of one throwing away anchors, plunged into the heart of his matter, and as he spoke the look on Mrs Makebelieve's face changed quickly from bewilderment to curiosity and dulled again to a blank amazement. After the first few sentences she half turned to Mary, but an obscure shame prevented her from searching out her daughter's eyes. It was borne quickly and painfully to her that Mary had not treated her fairly : there was a secret here with which a mother ought to have been trusted, and one which she could not believe Mary would have withheld from her; and so, gauging her child's feelings by her own, she steadfastly refused to look at her lest the shocked surprise in her eyes might lacerate the girl she loved, and who she knew must at the instant be in a sufficient agony. Undoubtedly the man was suggesting that he wanted to marry her daughter, and the unexpectedness of such a proposal left her mentally gaping; but that there must have been some preliminaries of meeting and courtship became obvious to her. Mary also listened to his remarks in a stupor. Was there no possibility at all of getting away from the man? A tenacity such as this seemed to her malignant. She had the feeling of one being pursued by some relentless and unscrupulous hunter. She heard him speaking through a cloud, and the only things really clear to her were the thoughts which she knew her mother must be thinking. She was frightened and ashamed, and the sullenness which is the refuge of most young people descended upon her like a darkness. Her face grew heavy and vacant, and she stared in front of her in the attitude of one who had nothing to do with what was passing. She did not believe altogether that he was in earnest : her immediate discomfort showed him as one who was merely seeking to get her into trouble with her mother in order to gratify an impotent rage. Twice or three times she flamed suddenly, went tiptoe to run from the room. A flash, and she would be gone from the place, down the stairs, into the streets, and away anywhere, and she tingled with the very speed of her vision; but she knew that one word from her mother would halt her like a barrier, and she hated the thought that he should be a witness to her obedience.

While he was speaking he did not look at Mary. He told Mrs Makebelieve that he loved her daughter very much, and he begged her permission and favour for his suit. He gave her to understand that he and Mary had many opportunities of becoming acquainted, and were at one in this desire for matrimony. To Mrs Makebelieve's mind there recurred a conversation which she had once held with her daughter, when Mary was curious to know if a policeman was a desirable person for a girl to marry. She saw this question now, not as being prompted by a laudable, an almost scientific curiosity, but as the interested, sly speculation of a schemer hideously accomplished in deceit. Mary could see that memory flitting back through her mother's brain, and it tormented her. Nor was her mother at ease—there was no chair to sit upon; she had to stand and listen to all this while he

110

spoke, more or less at his ease, from the bed. If she also had been sitting down she might have been mistress of her thoughts and able to deal naturally with the situation; but an easy pose is difficult when standing : her hands would fold in front of her, and the school-girl attitude annoyed and restrained her. Also, the man appeared to be in earnest in what he said. His words at the least, and the intention which drove them, seemed honourable. She could not give rein to her feelings without lapsing to a barbarity which she might not justify to herself even in anger, and might, indeed, blush to remember. Perhaps his chief disqualification consisted in a relationship to Mrs O'Connor for which he could not justly be held to blame, and for which she sincerely pitied him. But this certainly was a disqualification never to be redeemed. He might leave his work, or his religion, or his country, but he could never quit his aunt, because he carried her with him under his skin; he was her with additions, and at times Mrs Makebelieve could see Mrs O'Connor looking cautiously at her through the policeman's eyes; a turn of his forehead and she was there like a thin wraith that vanished and appeared again. The man was spoiled for her. He did not altogether lack sense, and the fact that he wished to marry her daughter showed that he was not so utterly beyond the reach of redemption as she had fancied.

Meanwhile, he had finished his statement as regarded the affection which he bore to her daughter and the suitability of their temperaments, and had hurled himself into an explanation of his worldly affairs, comprising his salary as a policeman, the possibility of promotion and the increased emoluments which would follow it, and the certain pension which would sustain his age. There were, furthermore, his parents, from whose decease he would reap certain monetary increments, and the deaths of other relatives from which an additional enlargement of his revenues might reasonably be expected. Indeed, he had not desired to speak of these matters at all, but the

stony demeanour of Mrs Makebelieve and the sullen aloofness of her daughter forced him, however reluctantly, to
draw even ignoble weapons from his armoury. He had
not conceived they would be so obdurate : he had, in fact,
imagined that the elder woman must be flattered by his
offer to marry her daughter, and when no evidence to
support this was forthcoming he was driven to appeal to
the cupidity which he believed occupies the heart of every
middle-aged, hard-worked woman. But these statements
also were received with a dreadful composure. He could
have smashed Mrs Makebelieve where she stood. Now
and again his body strained to a wild, physical outburst,
a passionate, red fury that would have terrified these
women to their knees, while he roared their screams into
thin whimpers as a man should. He did not even dare to
stop speaking, and his efforts at an easy, good-humoured,
half-careless presentation of his case was bitterly painful
to him as it was to his auditors. The fact that they were
both standing up unnerved him also—the pleasant
equality which should have formed the atmosphere of
such an interview was destroyed from the first moment,
and having once sat down, he did not like to stand up
again. He felt glued to the bed on which he sat, and he
felt also that if he stood up the tension in the room
would so relax that Mrs Makebelieve would at once
break out into speech sarcastic and final, or her daughter
might scream reproaches and disclaimers of an equal
finality. At her he did not dare to look, but the corner
of his eye could see her shape stiffened against the fireplace, an attitude so different from the pliable contours
to which he was accustomed in her as almost to be
repellent. He would have thanked God to find himself
outside the room, but how to get out of it he did not
know : his self-esteem forbade anything like a retreat
without honour, his nervousness did not permit him to
move at all, the anger which prickled the surface of his
body and mind was held in check only by an instinct of
fear as to what he might do if he moved, and so, with

112

dreadful jocularity, he commenced to speak of himself, his personal character, his sobriety and steadiness—of all those safe negations on which many women place reliance he spoke, and also of certain small vices which he magnified merely for the sake of talking, such as smoking, an odd glass of porter, and the shilling which, now and again, he had ventured upon a racehorse.

Mary listened to him for a while with angry intentness. The fact that she was the subject of his extraordinary discourse quickened at the first all her apprehensions. Had the matter been less important she would have been glad to look at herself in this strange position, and to savour, with as much detachment as was possible, the whole spirit of the adventure. But when she heard him, as she put it, 'telling on her', laying bare to her mother all the walks they had taken together, visits to restaurants and rambles through the streets and the parks, what he had said to her on this occasion and on that, and her remarks on such and such a matter, she could not visualise him save as a malignant and uncultivated person; and when he tacitly suggested that she was as eager for matrimony as he was, and so put upon her the horrible onus of rejecting him before a second person, she closed her mind and her ears against him. She refused to listen, although her perceptions admitted the trend of his speech. His words droned heavily and monotonously to her as through dull banks of fog. She made up her mind that if she were asked any questions by either of them she would not reply, and that she would not look at either of them; and then she thought that she would snap and stamp her feet and say that she hated him, that he had looked down on her because she worked for his aunt, that he had meanly been ashamed of and cut her because she was poor, that he had been going with another girl all the time he was going with her, and that he only pursued her in order to annoy her; that she didn't love him, that she didn't even like him—that, in fact, she disliked him heartily. She wished to say all these things in one whirling outcry, but feared that before she had rightly begun she might become abashed, or, worse, might burst into tears and lose all the dignity which she meant to preserve in his presence for the purpose of showing to him in the best light exactly what he was losing.

But the big man had come to the end of his speech. He made a few attempts to begin anew on the desirability of such a union for both of them, and the happiness it would give him if Mrs Makebelieve would come to live with them when they were married. He refused to let it appear that there was any doubt as to Mary's attitude in the matter, for up to the moment he came to their door he had not doubted her willingness himself. Her late avoidance of him he had put down to mere feminine tactics, which leads on by holding off. The unwilling person he had been assured was himself—he stooped to her, and it was only after a severe battle that he had been able to do it. The astonishment and disapproval of his relatives and friends at such a step were very evident to him, for to a man of his position and figure girls were cheap creatures, the best of them to be had for the mere asking. Therefore, the fact that this girl could be seriously rejecting his offer of marriage came upon him like red astonishment. He had no more to say, however, and he blundered and fumbled into silence.

For a moment or two the little room was so still that the quietness seemed to hum and buzz like an eternity. Then, with a sigh, Mrs Makebelieve spoke.

'I don't know at all,' said she, 'why you should speak to me about this, for neither my daughter nor yourself has ever even hinted to me before that you were courting one another. Why Mary should keep such a secret from her own mother I don't know. Maybe I've been cruel and frightened her, although I don't remember doing anything that she could have against me of that sort : or, maybe, she didn't think I was wise enough to advise her about a particular thing like her marriage, for, God

114

knows, old women are foolish enough in their notions, or else they wouldn't be slaving and grinding for the sake of their children the way they do be doing year in and year out, every day in the week, and every hour of the day. It isn't any wonder at all that a child would be a liar and a sleeveen and a trampler of the roads with the first man that nods to her when her mother is a foolish person that she can't trust. Of course, I wouldn't be looking for a gentleman like yourself to mention the matter to me when I might be scrubbing out your aunt's kitchen or her hall-door, maybe, and you sitting in the parlour with the company. Sure, I'm only an old char-woman, and what does it matter at all what I'd be thinking, or whether I'd be agreeing or not to anything? Don't I get my wages for my work, and what more does anybody want in the world? As for me going to live with you when you are married—it was kind of you to ask me that; but it's not the sort of thing I'm likely to do, for if I didn't care for you as a stranger I'm not going to like you any better as my daughter's husband. You'll excuse me saying one thing, sir, but while we are talk-ing we may as well be talking out, and it's this—that I never did like you, and I never will like you, and I'd sooner see my daughter married to any one at all than to yourself. But, sure, I needn't be talking about it; isn't it Mary's business altogether? and she'll be settling it with you nicely, I don't doubt. She's a practised hand now at arranging things, like you are yourself, and it will do me good to be learning something from her.'

Mrs Makebelieve took a cloth in her hand and walked over to the fireplace, which she commenced to polish.

The big man looked at Mary. It was incumbent on him to say something. Twice he attempted to speak, and each time, on finding himself about to say something regard-ing the weather, he stopped. Mary did not look at him; her eyes were fixed stubbornly on a part of the wall well away from his neighbourhood, and it seemed to him that she had made a vow to herself never to look at him again. But the utter silence of the room was unbearable. He knew that he ought to get up and go out, but he could not bring himself to do so. His self-love, his very physical strength, rebelled against so tame a surrender. One thought he gathered in from swaying vacuity—that the timid little creature whom he had patronised would not find the harsh courage to refuse him point-blank if he charged her straitly with the question : and so he again assayed speech.

'Your mother is angry with us, Mary,' said he, 'and I suppose she has good right to be angry; but the reason I did not speak to her before, as I admit I should have if I'd done the right thing, was that I had very few chances of meeting her, and never did meet her without some other person being there at the same time. I suppose the reason you did not say anything was that you wanted to be quite sure of yourself and of me too before you mentioned it. We have both done the wrong thing in not being open, but maybe your mother will forgive us when she knows we had no intention of hurting her, or of doing anything behind her back. Your mother seems to hate me : I don't know why, because she hardly knows me at all, and I've never done her any harm or said a word against her. Perhaps when she knows me as well as you do she'll change her mind : but you know I love you better than any one else, and that I'd do anything I could to please you and be a good husband to you. What I want to ask you before your mother is—will you marry me?'

Mary made no reply. She did not look or give the slightest sign that she had heard. But now it was that she did not dare to look at him. The spectacle of this big man badgered by her and by her mother, pleading to her, and pleading, as he and she well knew, hopelessly, would have broken her heart if she looked at him. She had to admire the good masculine fight he made of it. Even his tricks of word and tactic, which she instantly divined, moved her almost to tears; but she feared

116

terribly that if she met his gaze she might not be able
to resist his huge helplessness, and that she might be
compelled to do whatever he begged of her even in
despite of her own wishes.

The interval which followed his question weighed upon
them all. It was only broken by Mrs Makebelieve, who
began to hum a song as she polished the fire-grate. She
meant to show her careless detachment from the whole
matter, but in the face of Mary's silence she could not
keep it up. After a few moments she moved around and
said :

'Why don't you answer the gentleman, Mary?'

Mary turned and looked at her, and the tears which
she had resisted so long swam in her eyes; although she
could keep her features composed she had no further
command over her tears.

'I'll answer whatever you ask me, mother,' she whispered.

'Then, tell the gentleman whether you will marry him
or not.'

'I don't want to marry any one at all,' said Mary.

'You are not asked to marry any one, darling,' said
Mrs Makebelieve, 'but some one—this gentleman here
whose name I don't happen to know. Do you know his
name?'

'No,' said Mary.

'My name . . .' began the policeman.

'It doesn't matter, sir,' said Mrs Makebelieve. 'Do you
want to marry this gentleman, Mary?'

'No,' whispered Mary.

'Are you in love with him?'

Mary turned completely away from him.

'No,' she whispered again.

'Do you think you ever will be in love with him?'

She felt as a rat might when hunted to a corner. But
the end must be very near; this could not last for ever,
because nothing can. Her lips were parched, her eyes
were burning. She wanted to lie down and go asleep,

and waken again laughing to say, 'It was a dream.'

Her reply was almost inaudible. 'No,' she said.

'You are quite sure? It is always better to be quite sure.'

She did not answer any more, but the faint droop of her head gave the reply her mother needed

'You see, sir,' said Mrs Makebelieve, 'that you were mistaken in your opinion. My daughter is not old enough yet to be thinking of marriage and such-like. Children do be thoughtless. I am sorry for all the trouble she has given you, and'—a sudden compunction stirred her, for the man was standing up now, and there was no trace of Mrs O'Connor visible in him; his face was as massive and harsh as a piece of wall. 'Don't you be thinking too badly of us now,' said Mrs Makebelieve, with some agitation; 'the child is too young altogether to be asking her to marry. Maybe in a year or two—I said things, I know, but I was vexed, and . . .'.

The big man nodded his head and marched out.

Mary ran to her mother, moaning like a sick person, but Mrs Makebelieve did not look at her. She lay down on the bed and turned her face to the wall, and she did not speak to Mary for a long time.

31

When the young man who lodged with Mrs Cafferty came in on the following day he presented a deplorable appearance. His clothes were torn and his face had several large strips of sticking-plaster on it, but he seemed to be in a mood of extraordinary happiness notwithstanding, and proclaimed that he had participated in the one really great fight of his lifetime, that he wasn't injured at all, and that he wouldn't have missed it for a pension.

Mrs Cafferty was wild with indignation, and marched him into Mrs Makebelieve's room, where he had again to tell his story and have his injuries inspected and commiserated. Even Mr Cafferty came into the room on this occasion. He was a large, slow man, dressed very comfortably in a red beard—his beard was so red and so persistent that it quite overshadowed the rest of his wrappings and did, indeed, seem to clothe him. As he stood the six children walked in and out of his legs, and stood on his feet in their proper turns without causing him any apparent discomfort. During the young man's recital Mr Cafferty every now and then solemnly and powerfully smote his left hand with his right fist, and requested that the aggressor should be produced to him.

The young man said that as he was coming home the biggest man in the world walked up to him. He had never set eyes on the man before in his life, and thought at first he wanted to borrow a match or ask the way to somewhere, or something like that, and, accordingly, he halted; but the big man gripped him by the shoulder and said, 'You damned young whelp!' and then he laughed and hit him a tremendous blow with his other hand. He twisted himself free at that, and said, 'What's that for?' and then the big man made another desperate clout at him. A fellow wasn't going to stand that kind of thing, so he let out at him with his left, and then jumped in with two short arm jabs that must have tickled the chap; that fellow didn't have it all his own way anyhow. . . . The young man exhibited his knuckles, which were skinned and bleeding, as evidence of some exchange; but he averred, you might as well be punching a sack of coal as that man's face. In another minute they both slipped and rolled over and over in the road, hitting and kicking as they sprawled : then a crowd of people ran forward and pulled them asunder. When they were separated he saw the big man lift his fist, and the person who was holding him ducked suddenly and ran for his life : the other folk got out of the way too, and the big man

119

walked over to where he stood and stared into his face. His jaw was stuck out like the seat of a chair, and his moustache was like a bristle of barbed wire. The young man said to him, 'What the hell's wrong with you to go bashing a man for nothing at all?' and all of a sudden the big fellow turned and walked away. It was a grand fight altogether, said the youth, but the other man was a mile and a half too big for him.

As this story proceeded Mrs Makebelieve looked once or twice at her daughter. Mary's face had gone very pale, and she nodded back a confirmation of her mother's conjecture; but it did not seem necessary or wise to either of them that they should explain their thoughts. The young man did not require either condolences or revenge. He was well pleased at an opportunity to measure his hardihood against a worthy opponent. He had found that his courage exceeded his strength, as it always should—for how could we face the gods and demons of existence if our puny arms were not backed up by our invincible eyes?—and he displayed his contentment at the issue as one does a banner emblazoned with merits. Mrs Makebelieve understood also that the big man's action was merely his energetic surrender, as of one who, instead of tendering his sword courteously to the victor, hurls it at him with a malediction; and that in assaulting their friend he was bidding them farewell as heartily and impressively as he was able. So they fed the young man and extolled him, applauding to the shrill winding of his trumpet until he glowed again in the full satisfaction of heroism.

He and Mary did not discontinue their evening walks. Of these Mrs Makebelieve was fully cognisant, and although she did not remark on the fact, she had been observing the growth of their intimacy with a care which was one part approval and one part pain; for it was very evident to her that her daughter was no longer a child to be controlled and directed by authority. Her little girl was a big girl; she had grown up and was eager to undertake the business of life on her own behalf. But the period 'of Mrs Makebelieve's motherhood had drawn to a close, and her arms were empty. She was too used now to being a mother to relinquish easily the prerogatives of that status, and her discontent had this justification and assistance that it could be put into definite words, fronted and approved or rejected as reason urged. By knowledge and thought we will look through a stone wall if we look long enough, for we see less through eyes than through time. Time is the clarifying perspective whereby myopia of any kind is adjusted, and a thought emerges in its field as visibly, as a tree does in nature's. Mrs Makebelieve saw seventeen years' apprenticeship to maternity cancelled automatically without an explanation or a courtesy, and for a little time her world was in ruins, the ashes of existence powdered her hair and her forehead. Then she discovered that the debris was valuable in known currency; the dust was golden : her love remained to her undisturbed and unlikely to be disturbed by whatever event. And she discovered further that parentage is neither a game nor a privilege, but a duty! it is—astounding thought—the care of the young until the young can take care of itself. It was for this freedom only that her elaborate care had been necessary; her bud had blossomed and she could add no more to its bloom or fragrance. Nothing had happened that was not natural and whoso opposes his brow against that imperious urgency is thereby renouncing his kind and claiming a kinship with the wild boar and the goat, which they, too, may repudiate with leaden foreheads. There remained also the common human equality, not alone of blood, but of sex also, which might be fostered and grow to an intimacy more dear and enduring, more lovely and loving, than the necessarily one-sided devotions of parentage. Her duties in that relationship having been performed, it was her daughter's turn to take up hers and prove her rearing by repaying to her mother the conscious love which intelligence and a good heart dictates. This given, Mrs Makebelieve could smile happily again, for her arms would be empty only for a little time. The continuity of nature does not fail, saving for extraordinary instances. She sees to it that a breast and an arm shall not very long be unoccupied, and consequently, as Mrs Makebelieve sat contemplating that futurity which is nothing more than a prolongation of experience, she could smile contentedly, for all was very well.

32

If the unexpected did not often happen life would be a logical, scientific progression which might become dispirited and repudiate its goal for very boredom, but nature has cunningly diversified the methods whereby she coaxes or coerces us to prosecute, not our own, but her own adventure. Beyond every corner there may be a tavern or a church wherein both the saint and the sinner may be entrapped and remoulded. Beyond the skyline you may find a dynamite cartridge, a drunken tinker, a mad dog, or a shilling which some person has dropped; and any one of these unexpectednesses may be potent to urge the traveller down a side street and put a crook in the straight line which had been his life, and to which he had become miserably reconciled. The element of surprise being, accordingly, one of the commonest things in the world, we ought not to be hypercritical in our review of singularities, or say, 'These things do not happen'—because it is indisputable that they do happen. That combination which comprises a dark night, a highwayman armed and hatted to the teeth, and myself, may be a purely fortuitous one, but will such a criticism bring any comfort to the highwayman? And the concourse of three benevolent million-aires with the person to whom poverty can do no more is so pleasant and possible that I marvel it does not occur more frequently. I am prepared to believe on the very lightest assurance that these things do happen, but are hushed up for reasons which would be cogent enough if they were available.

Mrs Makebelieve opened the letter which the evening's post had brought to her. She had pondered well before opening it, and had discussed with her daughter all the possible people who could have written it. The envelope was long and narrow; it was addressed in a swift emphatic hand, the tail of the letter M enjoying a career distinguished beyond any of its fellows by length and beauty. The envelope, moreover, was sealed by a brilliant red lion with jagged whiskers and a simper, who threatened the person daring to open a missive not addressed to him with the vengeance of a battle-axe which was balanced lightly but truculently on his right claw.

This envelope contained several documents purport-ing to be copies of extraordinary originals, and amongst them a letter which was read by Mrs Makebelieve more than ten thousand times or ever she went to bed that night. It related that more than two years previously one Patrick Joseph Brady had departed this life, and that his will (dated from a multitudinous address in New York) devised and bequeathed to his dearly beloved sister Mary Eileen Makebelieve, otherwise Brady, the following shares and securities for shares, to wit . . . and the thereinafter mentioned houses and mes-suages, lands, tenements, hereditaments, and premises, that was to say . . . and all household furniture, books, pictures, prints, plate, linen, glass, and objects of vertu, carriages, wines, liquors, and all consumable stores and effects whatsoever then in the house so and so, and all money then in the bank and thereafter to accrue due upon the thereinbefore mentioned stocks, funds, shares,

and securities. . . . Mrs Makebelieve wept and besought
God not to make a fool of a woman who was not only
poor but old. The letter requested her to call on the following day, or at her earliest convenience, to 'the above
address', and desired that she should bring with her
such letters or other documents as would establish her
relationship to the deceased and assist in extracting the
necessary Grant of Probate to the said Will, and it was
subscribed by Messrs Platitude and Gamble, Solicitors,
Commissioners for Oaths, and Protectors of the Poor.

To the Chambers of these gentlemen Mrs Makebelieve
and Mary repaired on the following day, and having produced the letters and other documents for inspection,
the philanthropists, Platitude and Gamble, professed
themselves to be entirely satisfied as to their *bona fides*,
and exhibited an eagerness to be of immediate service
to the ladies in whatever capacity might be conceived.
Mrs Makebelieve instantly invoked the Pragmatic Sanc-
tion; she put the entire matter to the touchstone of
absolute verity by demanding an advance of fifty pounds.
Her mind reeled as she said the astounding amount, but
her voice did not. A cheque was signed and a clerk des-
patched, who returned with eight five-pound notes and
ten sovereigns of massy gold. Mrs Makebelieve secreted
these, and went home marvelling to find that she was yet
alive. No trams ran over her. The motor-cars pursued
her, and were evaded. She put her hope in God, and
explained so breathlessly to the furious street. One
cyclist who took corners on trust she cursed by the
Ineffable Name, but instantly withdrew the malediction
for luck, and addressed his dwindling back with an eye
of misery and a voice of benediction. For a little time
neither she nor her daughter spoke of the change in
their fortunes saving in terms of allusion; they feared
that, notwithstanding their trust, God might hear and
shatter them with His rolling laughter. They went out
again that day furtively and feverishly and bought. . . .

But on the following morning Mrs Makebelieve

returned again to her labour. She intended finishing her
week's work with Mrs O'Connor (it might not last for
a week). She wished to observe that lady with the exact
particularity, the singleness of eye, the true, candid, critical scrutiny which had hitherto been impossible to her.
It was, she said to Mary, just possible that Mrs O'Connor
might make some remarks about soap. It was possible
that the lady might advance theories as to how this or
that particular kind of labour ought to be conducted.
. . . Mrs Makebelieve's black eyes shone upon her child
with a calm peace, a benevolent happiness rare indeed
to human regard.

In the evening of that day Mary and the young man
who lodged with their neighbour went out for the walk
which had become customary with them. The young
man had been fed with an amplitude which he had never
known before, so that not even the remotest slim thread,
shred, hint, echo, or memory of hunger remained with
him : he tried but could not make a dint in himself
anywhere, and, consequently, he was as sad as only a
well-fed person can be. Now that his hunger was gone
he deemed that all else was gone also. His hunger, his
sweetheart, his hopes, his good looks (for his injuries
had matured to the ripe purple of the perfect bruise), all
were gone, gone, gone. He told it to Mary, but she did
not listen to him; to the rolling sky he announced it, and
it paid no heed. He walked beside Mary at last in silence,
listening to her plans and caprices, the things she would
do and buy, the people to whom gifts should be made,
and the species of gift uniquely suitable to this person
and to that person, the people to whom money might be
given and the amounts, and the methods whereby such
largesse could be distributed. Hats were mentioned, and
dresses, and the new house somewhere—a space-
embracing somewhere, beyond surmise, beyond geog-
raphy. They walked onwards for a long time, so long
that at last a familiar feeling stole upon the youth. The
word 'food' seemed suddenly a topic worthy of the most

spirited conversation. His spirits arose. He was no longer
solid, space belonged to him also, it was in him and of
him, and so there was a song in his heart. He was hungry
and the friend of man again. Now everything was possible. The girl? Was she not by his side? The regenera-
tion of Ireland and of Man? That could be done also;
a little leisure and everything that can be thought can be
done : even his good looks might be returned to him; he
felt the sting and tightness of his bruises and was reas-
sured, exultant. He was a man predestined to bruises;
they would be his meat and drink and happiness, his
refuge and sanctuary for ever. Let us leave him, then,
pacing volubly by the side of Mary, and exploring with
a delicate finger his half-closed eye, which, until it was
closed entirely, would always be half-closed by the
decent buffer of misfortune. His ally and stay was hunger, and there is no better ally for any man : that satisfied and the game is up; for hunger is life, ambition,
goodwill and understanding, while fullness is all those
negatives which culminate in greediness, stupidity, and
decay; so his bruises troubled him no further than as
they affected the eyes of a lady wherein he prayed to be
comely.

Bruises, unless they are desperate indeed, will heal at
the last for no other reason than that they must. The
inexorable compulsion of all things is towards health or
destruction, life or death, and we hasten our joys or our
woes to the logical extreme. It is urgent, therefore, that
we be joyous if we wish to live. Our heads may be as
solid as is possible, but our hearts and our heels shall be
light or we are ruined. As to the golden mean—let us
have nothing to do with that thing at all; it may only be
gilded, it is very likely made of tin of a dull colour and
a lamentable sound, unworthy even of being stolen; and
unless our treasures may be stolen they are of no use
to us. It is contrary to the laws of life to possess that
which other people do not want; therefore, your beer
shall foam, your wife shall be pretty, and your little

truth shall have a plum in it—for this is so, that your beer can only taste of your company, you can only know your wife when some one else does, and your little truth shall be savoured or perish. Do you demand a big truth? Then, O Ambitious! you must turn aside from all your companions and sit very quietly, and if you sit long enough and quiet enough it may come to you; but this thing alone of all things you cannot steal, nor can it be given to you by the County Council. It cannot be communicated, and yet you may get it. It is unspeakable but not unthinkable, and it is born as certainly and unaccountably as you were yourself, and is of just as little immediate consequence. Long, long ago, in the dim beginnings of the world, there was a careless and gay young man who said, 'Let truth go to hell'—and it went there. It was his misfortune that he had to follow it; it is ours that we are his descendants. An evil will either kill you or be killed by you, and (the reflection is comforting) the odds are with us in every fight waged against humanity by the dark or elemental beings. But humanity is timid and lazy, a believer in golden means and subterfuges and compromises, loath to address itself to any combat until its frontiers are virtually overrun and its cities and granaries and places of refuge are in jeopardy from those gloomy marauders. In that wide struggle which we call progress, evil is always the aggressor and the vanquished, and it is right that this should be so, for without its onslaughts and depredations humanity might fall to a fat slumber upon its cornsacks and die snoring : or, alternatively, lacking these valorous alarms and excursions, it might become self-satisfied and formularised, and be crushed to death by the mere dull density of virtue. Next to good the most valuable factor in life is evil. By the interaction of these all things are possible, and therefore (or for any other reason that pleases you) let us wave a friendly hand in the direction of that bold, bad policeman whose thoughts were not governed by the Book of Regulations which is issued to all recruits, and who, in despite of the fact that he was enrolled among the very legions of order, had that chaos in his soul which may 'give birth to a Dancing Star'.

As to Mary: even ordinary, workaday politeness frowns on too abrupt a departure from a lady, particularly one whom we have companioned thus distantly from the careless simplicity of girlhood to the equally careless but complex businesses of adolescence. The world is all before her, and her chronicler may not be her guide. She will have adventures, for everybody has. She will win through with them, for everybody does. She may even meet bolder and badder men than the policeman—shall we, then, detain her? I, for one, having urgent calls elsewhere, will salute her fingers and raise my hat and stand aside, and you will do likewise, because it is my pleasure that you should. She will go forward, then, to do that which is pleasing to the gods, for less than that she cannot do, and more is not to be expected of any one.

: : : *Thus far the story of Mary Makebelieve*